W9-AXC-036

MURDER IN MORRILL
B. H. B. Harper

Claire Markham has a new job and an absent fiancé. As the newest hire of the English Department at Oklahoma State University, she finds the job overwhelming. It's difficult to keep her mind on her work when her handsome fiancé, an actor, is on location in Italy, and his calls are growing less frequent. However, Claire has a more immediate problem. A colleague has been murdered, and his missing briefcase is found hidden in her locked office.

The cold-eyed police investigator has labeled her "a person of interest." Claire had means and an opportunity; all she lacks is a motive, and Captain Garrison is eager to establish one for her. To exonerate herself, Claire attempts to find the murderer herself. Her search leads her into campus politics, departmental conflicts, faculty secrets, and the arms of the dead man's rugged son, as well as the hands of the killer.

MURDER IN MORRILL

•

B. H. B. Harper

AVALON BOOKS
NEW YORK

Published by Thomas Bouregy & Co., Inc.
160 Madison Avenue, New York, NY 10016

Library of Congress Cataloging-in-Publication Data

Harper, B. H. B. (Bena Harlene Brewer)
   Murder in Morrill / B.H.B. Harper.
      p. cm.
   ISBN 978-0-8034-9979-9
   1. Women college teachers—Fiction.   2. Oklahoma State
University—Fiction.   3. Murder—Investigation—Fiction.
I. Title.

PS3608.A77M87 2009
813'.6—dc22

                                        2009012802

PRINTED IN THE UNITED STATES OF AMERICA
ON ACID-FREE PAPER
BY HADDON CRAFTSMEN, BLOOMSBURG, PENNSYLVANIA

For Brittany Marie and Evalyn Rose—Go for it, ladies!

Chapter One

The door to the dark hall jerked ajar. A glittering eye peered through the narrow crack. Behind that glittering eye, a frantic mind raced.

I can't believe that happened! It was so quick! I've got to get out of here; I . . . I . . .

Although stunned, the mind held the body in check, and the dark figure behind the door, fighting a blind urge to run, took a deep breath. The mind steadied and focused.

Easy . . . easy. Got to be careful. I can't be seen. Especially not now.

The door inched open, and the shadow cautiously half-stepped into the hall, listening. The broad third-floor hall in the aged-brick campus building was empty. Ambient light from the tall window in the east stairwell of Morrill Hall shone dully on the tile floor. The figure glanced back into the unlit office.

Okay. What's done is done. No one knows I've been here. But I still don't have what I came for. Those things weren't in the desk or filing cabinet, so they must be in his briefcase. I can't stay here to check it. I'll have to take it with me.

The shadowy form bent and picked up the heavy briefcase that had been dropped just inside the office door.

I hadn't expected that to happen tonight. But I had no choice. What was the old fool doing up here this late anyway? He shouldn't have been here.

But the old fool had come in, and what wasn't expected to happen had happened. And now it was imperative that the late-night intruder leave the building without being seen.

The black silhouette stepped into the hall and shut the windowless office door firmly, testing the knob to be sure it locked. The figure cocked an ear toward the elevator, listening for the hum of the motor that would indicate if anyone else was stirring in the building.

The custodians are always gone by this time, but it's possible some graduate student might be coming to that office of theirs. You never know when those kids are going to be around they keep such crazy hours, but good— I don't hear the elevator.

Assured no one else was in the building, the figure quickly glided to the east staircase and hurried silently down to the second-floor landing. There the intruder paused to consider another potential problem.

Someone might be outside. I can't be seen leaving with a briefcase, not tonight anyway. But I don't need to take it. All I need is to find someplace in the building where I can go through it.

The figure turned into the dark hallway of the second floor, which was lit only by a red exit sign, and stopped at the first door. Shifting the heavy briefcase from the right to the left hand, the dark form reached into a jacket pocket for the small flashlight.

It's gone! I must have dropped it when I grabbed . . . Crud! *It's up there in his office.*

The figure looked back at the stairwell to the third floor and considered returning for the flashlight.

I can't take time to go after it. I need to get out of here. But not before I've checked his briefcase.

The intruder turned again to the door, once more fumbling in a jacket pocket, this time finding what was sought.

Handy thing, a master key, and no one knows I have it.

The key was quickly inserted into the lock, and the door opened quietly. Swiftly the shadowy form entered the dark room, closed the door, and stood in the office directly below the one just vacated on the floor above.

The intruder moved forward and with a curse stumbled into something heavy.

Blast it! What the—Oh, right. Boxes all over the

place. Isn't that stupid woman ever going to unpack? How could anyone work in such a mess?

The figure paused long enough for the glittering eyes to adjust to the faint glow that seeped in around the edges of the venetian blind that blocked most of the light thrown by a street lamp outside the large south window. The intruder's gloved hand, reaching for the light switch, halted on the toggle.

Wait a minute! If light can get in, it can also get out. An office light on this late might be noticed by the campus police. If an officer came to check . . . No, I can't risk that. But too much has happened to stop now.

The fertile mind raced.

This isn't the only door the key will open. There's that odd room on the ground floor. The one directly behind the big flight of concrete steps out front. Those stairs block its south wall and that room is windowless, so no light can be seen from the outside there. That's where I should have gone instead of opening the first door I came to. Glad I thought of it now.

Just as the figure stepped into the hall, the sound of an outside door opening echoed up the stairwell. The intruder froze in place, hand still on the office doorknob, heart racing. Loud male voices, bemoaning research papers that needed to be written and essays that needed to be graded, indicated the intruder was no longer alone. A couple of graduate teaching assistants had just entered the building. The figure edged back into the cluttered room and shut the door softly. The complaining voices moved down the ground floor hallway toward the English graduate office. The dark shape behind the closed door swore in frustration.

Just because they're in the grad office doesn't mean they'll stay there. Last week a bunch of them were caught playing hacky sack out in the hall at midnight.

There was no way the intruder could reach the windowless room where the briefcase could be examined without the chance of being seen by the new arrivals. Nor could the dark figure safely leave the building with the briefcase. Especially if other grad students started showing up.

If only I had that flashlight, I could check the briefcase in here, but I don't. It won't be long before they'll discover his briefcase is missing, and when they do, they'll start looking for who took it. So I can't be seen carrying it off tonight. What can I do? Think! Think!

The agitated mind didn't like its only option, but there seemed to be no choice.

If I can't check the briefcase now or take it with me, there's only one thing I can do. It's a gamble, but I'll have to leave it here. It's bad enough if I'm seen, and it would be worse if I'm seen with it. I'll have to hide it in here someplace. Someplace where it won't be found. Someplace where I can get it later.

The glittering eyes could scarcely make out the shapes of the furniture in the unlit office as they scanned the dark, cluttered room for a hiding place. Gradually a grim smile twisted the cruel mouth.

Maybe all this mess works to my advantage. Who'd notice one more thing in this hopeless jumble?

The intruder moved past the desk to the metal filing cabinet and found it shoved so tightly in a corner there wasn't room between it and the wall. Nor was there room for a briefcase in any drawer in the unlocked cabinet. Stacks of file folders haphazardly filled the drawers, and moving them to make room for the briefcase would only call attention to the very thing the intruder sought to conceal. The dark figure turned from the file cabinet and stepped to the two metal office chairs that held boxes of unshelved books in the hope of finding space in a partially filled box. But neither the boxes on the chairs nor those stacked on the floor before the empty bookshelves had room for the briefcase.

I can't just set it behind a stack of boxes. That won't work. Not tomorrow. Not when it's light. She'd be bound to notice it. She may be messy but she's not blind.

The glittering eyes swept the room once again as the gloved hand absently patted the jacket pocket that held the master key.

Slow down and think. There's got to be someplace in here big enough to hide this briefcase until I can get back.

Then those gleaming eyes stopped on the perfect hiding place, one that had been missed in the intruder's haste. The grim smile widened.

Morrill Hall was one of the oldest buildings on the Oklahoma State University campus, so old that fireplaces had once graced several of the offices in the structure.

This office was one of those so accoutred. But rather than having the opening paneled over as so often was done, some former occupant had enjoyed the cozy touch the fireplace lent. Although the flue was permanently closed, a stack of artificial logs lay on the tarnished grate of the defunct fireplace. This homey touch was almost obscured by the two chairs piled with boxes of books set in front of it.

The glittering eyes rested on the unused and unappreciated fireplace. Then the chairs were silently moved aside. It was an awkward reach, but between the artificial logs and the back of the deep firebox was just enough room for the briefcase. The leather case was settled tightly into place, and the chairs returned in front of the grate. The figure nodded with satisfaction. The briefcase, masked by the artificial logs, was so far back it would be difficult to see. The task completed, the intruder paused at the door, listening. All was quiet. Then, leaving the room as soundlessly as it had come, the figure checked the door to be sure the lock had engaged. In the hall the dark form hesitated once more, straining to hear the grad students or the elevator. The silence continued unbroken. Apparently the students were at work behind a closed door, and the elevator was idle.

The dark figure shunned the main doors of the stately old building, which opened south onto a pillared porch and a wide sweep of concrete steps that led down a full story to the street below. One would be too much on view there. Rather, the stealthy form returned to the east stairwell and continued down to the ground floor and out into the cold November night.

Once outside, the figure again checked the urge to run, knowing undue haste would call attention should anyone be crossing the campus at this late hour. The gloved hands turned up the collar of a brown jacket against the cold November wind. Then, the late-night visitor to Morrill Hall walked slowly across the empty parking lot. Should anyone be around to notice, all he would see was just another tired professor headed home after a long night's work, empty-handed.

And that's just what I'm doing. I'm going home after a late night's work. Granted, the work involved more than I expected. But it was something I was going to have to do, if not tonight then another night soon. It's just as well it's over.

The dark figure stopped beside a blue Saturn parked at the north end of the lot, unlocked the car, slid in, and drove away, while in his third-floor office in Morrill Hall, Dr. William Rhodes lay sprawled in a pool of blood, a letter opener protruding from his left carotid artery.

Chapter Two

Claire Markham was late for her appointment. The chestnut-haired young professor had been delayed by three students who had stayed after class to ask about their research papers—papers that were due the first of December—so she hurried from the Classroom Building back to Morrill Hall. She had no idea why Dr. Rhodes wanted to see her; she scarcely knew the man. She hoped he wasn't going to try to enlist her support in the inter-departmental war currently going on among the English faculty.

Apparently several running battles had begun long before she had been hired. They seemed to involve both a power struggle over the staffing of the graduate classes and the attempts of the literature professors to dissociate the department from its technical writing component.

Tied to these conflicts was a fight over which of the three junior faculty members coming up for an employment decision in the spring would or would not be granted tenure. Claire, a new hire and the most junior member in the English department, had deliberately avoided taking sides or even really trying to understand what the conflicts were all about. She had no intention of making enemies in the divided faculty. Politics and conflict were a given in any large department, and in three years they'd be making a tenure decision on her. Yet when she had found a note in her departmental mailbox from Dr. Rhodes, full professor and star departmental scholar, asking her to drop in after her Tuesday morning class for "a little visit" on some as yet unnamed subject, Claire didn't feel she could refuse.

Because she was late, Claire didn't take time to stop at her second-floor office, and because the elevator was both in use and slow, she took the stairs to the third floor and Dr. Rhodes' office. At the first landing she overtook Elaine Evans, the director of the freshman composition program and the nearest thing to a close friend Claire had on the faculty. In addition to her teaching responsibilities as basic course director, the petite brunette was responsible for the training and supervising of the thirty-seven graduate students who taught freshman comp, all of whom were taller and some older than she. Hers was a demanding and underappreciated job, and she handled it with a blend of topflight competence and friendly fairness.

"Hi, Claire," Elaine greeted her. "Where are you headed in such a hurry? Your face is all flushed."

"I was supposed to meet Dr. Rhodes fifteen minutes ago," she gasped, grimacing at the stitch that had just developed in her side.

"Well, slow down and catch your breath. You're already late; you don't want to be all sweaty and panty too."

Claire grinned at her friend. "You're right. What difference is a few more minutes going to make? I might as well be hung for a sheep as a lamb."

"Speaking of being hung, is this your turn for one of his 'little visits'?" Elaine asked as the two women continued up the wide stairs at a slower pace.

"I guess so. That's what his note said. Do you have any idea what it's about?" Claire asked.

"Not really, but he's been having several of the newer faculty members in, and none of them have left his office looking happy. George Karns—he's in technical writing—was overheard swearing under his breath when he left. I saw Geraldine Kosvoski storm out of his office in tears."

"Really? The world literature professor?" Claire asked, surprised. "She doesn't strike me as the crying type."

"She's not. Those were angry tears. She was furious. And yesterday Sydney Andrews, your buddy in American lit—"

"He's no buddy of mine," Claire corrected her teasing friend.

"Anyway, he looked absolutely grim when he left.

I've not been summoned yet, but I imagine I soon will be, since, along with Karns and Kosvoski, I'm up for a tenure decision this spring."

Claire recalled Elaine's fear that Dr. Rhodes would tell her that since the job of basic course director offered no opportunities for serious research, and thus produced no publications, she would not get his vote for tenure. Dr. Larkin, the department head, seemed pleased with her work, but Elaine had reason to believe his good opinion was not shared by Dr. Rhodes, and she dreaded his expected invitation for a "little visit."

Maybe Elaine hadn't been summoned yet, but Claire had been, and she was late for that appointment. As she waved good-bye to her friend she wondered if, like the three before her, she would be grimly swearing between sobs when she left Dr. Rhodes' office today.

By the time she reached his office door, her breathing had evened out, but she felt sweat gathering at the nape of her neck. She pushed a heavy lock of damp hair back from her forehead and glanced at her watch. She was eighteen minutes late. She turned the knob and frowned. The door was locked. She rapped on the door. No answer. She knocked again and waited. Still no answer. She was neither relieved or annoyed. Instead, the young woman suffered a moment of déjà vu.

Only fourteen months ago she had stood at another professor's door on another campus, her knock unanswered, despite her scheduled appointment. A little shiver ran down her spine at the memory. A fatal heart attack had kept Professor Coe Comfort from that appointment. As Claire turned from Dr. Rhodes' door and back to the stairs and her own office, she reminded herself this was Oklahoma State University in Stillwater, not Southwestern College in Winfield, Kansas. A death one place certainly did not portend a death at another. Undoubtedly something more important than a meeting with the newest member of the faculty, who was late, was claiming Dr. Rhodes' attention. She heard he'd just begun a two-year editorship of the prestigious English journal *The Oracle*. Maybe he was unexpectedly tied up with that. She'd call him later, she determined, to let him know she had tried to keep their appointment.

Shortly before lunch, Claire phoned Rhodes' office, but he didn't answer. Claire frowned. Although she wasn't eager to meet with him, she didn't want to be seen as careless, irresponsible, or indifferent, especially to the request of a senior and influential faculty member. Unable to contact him directly, she called the main English office and asked Sue Gooden, the departmental secretary, to put a note in his mailbox saying she had tried to reach him. The secretary complied but with an abruptness that bordered on rudeness. Not for the first time, Claire wondered if she had done something to offend the redheaded woman. Sue didn't treat Elaine or anyone else in that manner. But Claire quickly forgot Sue and her attitude as she set about preparing for her Children's Lit class.

When Dr. Rhodes didn't return her call that afternoon,

Claire was relieved. She intended to stay out of departmental politics. Of course, maybe he had only wanted to question her about her own scholarly work in which she had exposed Coe Z. Comfort, the assumed author of a series of much-loved children's books, as a fraud and plagiarizer. But whatever the reason, Claire was pleased he didn't call.

She wasn't so pleased, however, with her office, and she grumbled under her breath as she rummaged through an unpacked box, looking in vain for a book she needed. Everything was still where she had dumped it when she arrived on campus shortly before the fall semester began. Until now, her time had been consumed preparing lectures for her new classes and working on a convention submission. Consequently, the desk was where the former occupant had left it, in a spot that forced her to sit in her own shadow. The bookshelves that filled the north wall were still empty, while a number of boxes, mostly containing books, were sitting around on the chairs and the floor waiting to be unpacked. And it was stupid to have chairs blocking the view of what could be the most attractive feature in the room—the fireplace.

Several of the English faculty had let her know, rather enviously, that she had been given the prime office space only because of the notoriety her first book—the exposé of the plagiarizing writer—had received, and if seniority had any weight and there were a

God in heaven, she'd be working at a carrel in a crowded room with three other junior faculty members.

Claire knew her recently published dissertation was the reason she had been hired, and if that book was also the reason for the roomy office, she was grateful. And being grateful, she really should try to make the most of the coveted space. She wouldn't put it off any longer. Now that her apartment was finally in order, she would come back to the campus that night and see what she could do to improve things there, she decided. Perhaps in the evening she could work uninterrupted. There wouldn't be so many people about to drop in unexpectedly.

Lately several colleagues had taken to stopping by her office to visit, and the visitors all seemed to get around to their positions on the interdepartmental war, trying to elicit her support. Several were not shy about bad-mouthing Dr. Rhodes and Dr. Millington, two of the professors on the graduate faculty. Yesterday Lee Burrows, who taught linguistics, had stopped by long enough to put in a good word for Geraldine Kosvoski and Elaine Evans, and a bad one for George Karns. And George Karns, the lanky technical writing professor who had been seen angrily leaving Rhodes' office, and David Stands, a professor of British literature, had been by that day. Sydney Andrews, the short, broad-shouldered fellow American literature professor with a thick mustache and thinning brown hair, had stopped by both in the morning and the afternoon. Although departmental problems were the initial subject of his visits, Sydney seemed to be flirting more than seriously trying to elicit her support. If so, he was wasting his time, Claire laughed to herself. A diamond as large as that on her left hand discouraged most men, she thought with a smile, and the smile warmed and widened at the memory of the tall, golden-eyed, honey-haired actor who had put it there. The smile began to slip. Work had taken her fiancé, Dirk Drummond, to Italy in early August, and he wasn't due back until mid-December. Might he call this evening before she returned to campus to put her office in order? she wondered. As she entertained that wistful thought, Elaine, the petite freshman comp director, stopped at her open office door with a question that reflected Claire's own concern.

"I'm on my way home, but I wanted to ask before I left: Did Dirk call last night?"

"Hi, Elaine. No," Claire answered, "but I did get an e-mail." It had been a short, perfunctory message: a quick update on the filming schedule and a promise to call soon. However, the time difference between Italy and Oklahoma made calling when both were free difficult, Claire told herself. At least she hoped that was the reason his calls had been becoming more infrequent. She and Dirk had met last fall when she was doing research for her dissertation in the Kansas college town where he had taught between acting jobs. Maybe it had been a bad idea to fall in love with the handsome college department head/actor who had hired her as a last-minute substitute in freshman composition. But then, common sense had nothing to do with falling in love.

"Of course, you could pick up the phone and call him," Elaine reminded her.

"I could, but his schedule is more irregular than mine. I wouldn't want to bother him while he's on the set."

"Well, don't give up on him," Elaine ordered. "Wish I could stay and visit, but I've got to run. Jack and I are going to Tulsa for dinner tonight."

"Sounds like fun. Any special reason?"

"Yes. We're celebrating our anniversary. Doesn't seem possible we've been married three years. Time flies when you're having fun," she said with a grin.

And that was the kind of fun Claire was beginning to wonder if she would ever have. Italy was a long way from Oklahoma. She feared the old adage might be wrong. Maybe absence didn't make the heart grow fonder. Maybe absence allowed the eye to wander. She tried to keep her growing misgivings to herself, but Elaine sensed her concern.

"And, Claire, don't sweat it. He'll probably call tonight," her friend said just before she left.

Claire did have a call that evening, but not from Dirk. A distraught girlfriend from graduate school was having man trouble and called Claire for consolation and advice. Consequently, Claire's trip back to her campus office was delayed. Dressed in jeans and a sweatshirt, she finally made it to Morrill Hall prepared to spend as much time as necessary to make the most of her coveted office. To her surprise, the building was ablaze with lights. A custodial crew was working its way from the first floor on up to the second and third, waxing the floors of the halls, offices, and classrooms. Claire scowled with annoyance.

"Sorry, ma'am. Didn't Dr. Larkin tell you? We're scheduled to do Morrill tonight," a heavyset custodian greeted her as she started up the stairs.

"No. I guess I missed that e-mail."

"I'm afraid we'll be in your way, mopping and waxing, and those buffers are real loud. Ah—we'd hoped we'd have the building to ourselves."

The custodian couldn't order her out, but he plainly wanted her to take the hint and go. As he said, the crew might be in her way, and as he implied, she surely would be in theirs.

"Oh, sure. I can wait, and the floors can really use the attention. But when you get to my office, you're going to find a lot of boxes sitting around. Just move them however you need to," she said, smiling at the worried janitor before she turned for the outside door.

So the job she had put off for so long would have to be delayed a bit longer. However, a newly waxed floor would be nice. Besides, the coming weekend was Thanksgiving break. She would organize her office after she got back from the holiday dinner at her parents' home in Wichita. In fact, that exercise would help her work off her mother's candied yams and pumpkin pie, she decided.

Claire was not the only person whose interest in her office was hindered by the custodians' night-waxing duties. Long after she had left Morrill Hall, a figure in a brown jacket, cursing softly, turned away from the building and walked to a blue Saturn parked at the west end of the lot.

But Claire Markham's plans for the fall holiday were to be thwarted. She would enjoy neither Thanksgiving dinner in Wichita with her parents nor rearrange her office as she intended. She wouldn't be allowed out of Stillwater or into her office that weekend.

Chapter Three

"Where have you been? Captain Garrison's been asking for you."

Claire, startled, stared up into Sydney Andrews' concerned face as he opened her car door for her. Sydney, who had tried flirtatiously and unsuccessfully to engage her in whatever skulduggery was currently going on in the English department, looked at her with an anxious frown, his mouth taut under his thick mustache. He wasn't flirting now.

"I've been at my apartment. Why? And who is Captain Garrison?" she asked, bewildered as she stepped from her Ford Mustang. Her green eyes looked past the worried Sydney to the police cars in the Morrill Hall parking lot and the crowd milling at the east doorway, which was blocked by police officers.

"You mean you haven't heard? It's been on the radio and all the TV channels! And Larkin's been trying to reach you!" Sydney exclaimed.

It was Claire's turn to frown, noticing for the first time the TV trucks from every station in both Tulsa and Oklahoma City. What were they doing here, and why would Dr. Larkin, the department head, be trying to reach her so early in the morning? It wasn't even 8 yet, and she didn't have a class until nine thirty.

"I haven't had the news on, and Dr. Larkin must have called either while I was in the shower or right after I left for the campus. Why are all the police here?"

"The crew that was in here waxing floors last night found Dr. Rhodes dead in his office."

"Really?" Claire gasped. "That's terrible. But why all the police?"

"Apparently he was murdered."

"Murdered! Why would they think that?" Claire exclaimed.

"I suppose the letter opener in his neck was the first clue."

Sydney's flip remark and slightly sarcastic tone caused Claire to refocus her attention from the crowd at the east door of Morrill Hall back to the associate professor who had met her in the parking lot as she arrived. Aware of her sharp look and deepening frown, Sydney hastened to explain.

"Well, anyway, that's the buzz; that's what I heard when I got here."

Claire nodded her understanding as she tried to absorb Sydney's news. If memory served, Sydney was one of those in the small faction that opposed the group Dr. Rhodes seemed to be heading—or had headed, Claire quickly corrected to herself. She was having difficulty accepting the fact that the full professor of Elizabethan and Jacobean literature was dead. Dr. Rhodes had always struck her as pompous and condescending but not a candidate for murder.

"All English classes have been canceled for the day. The police are interviewing everyone who's officed in Morrill Hall and then sending us home. I've already been interviewed. But for some reason they've been particularly asking for you," Sydney said, looking at her closely.

"Whatever for? I scarcely knew Dr. Rhodes."

"Yeah. Me too, and I've been here four years. Well, good luck. The interview's not so bad. And this does mean we'll be starting Thanksgiving break a day early," he added as Claire started for the redbrick building.

"But who wants an extra day at that price?" Claire muttered to herself on her way across the parking lot to Morrill Hall.

She gave her name to the campus police officer at the east door, and he allowed her inside. There she was met by another officer who escorted her to the second-floor classroom where fellow faculty members and graduate teaching assistants, apparently waiting to be interviewed, sat in little knots, whispering among themselves. Elaine

Evans beckoned her over and motioned to an empty chair.

"Claire, isn't this awful? Dr. Rhodes was murdered! Who would do such a thing?" the petite woman exclaimed as Claire joined her.

"I can't believe it. I saw Sydney just now out in the parking lot, and he told me about it. When did it happen? Last night?" Claire asked as she loosened the long green scarf looped around her neck and unbuttoned her brown jacket.

"That's when he was found, although apparently he'd been there for a while, maybe as long as the night before. I heard that—"

Whatever Elaine had heard was interrupted by a frowning police officer carrying a clipboard.

"Has Dr. Claire Markham gotten here yet?" he asked impatiently.

All the conversations stopped as Claire rose.

"Yes, I'm here."

"Good. If you will come with me, please," he said, turning to the hall.

Claire followed the officer as every eye in the room followed her trim figure. The officer led her across the hall to the main English office.

"Captain Garrison will see you in here," he said, indicating the door to Dr. Larkin's office. Apparently the department head had surrendered his office to the campus police. "This is Dr. Markham, sir," he said before closing the door behind him.

The captain turned from the window and stared at Claire for a disturbing moment before speaking.

"Please have a seat, Dr. Markham. I'm Captain Grant Garrison of the OSU police. I'd like to ask you a few preliminary questions, if you don't mind."

Although the officer looked casual, dressed in chinos, a tweed jacket, and open-necked shirt, there was nothing casual in his manner, and Claire had the distinct impression he'd ask his questions even if she did mind.

"All right," she answered. The captain wasn't sitting, and Claire didn't either. "Is there some special reason you wanted to see me?" she asked.

"Yes, there is. You've heard, of course, about Dr. Rhodes." Once more he gestured her to the green office chair positioned before Dr. Larkin's desk, and once more she continued to stand.

"Only just now. Just when I got to campus a few minutes ago."

"You hadn't heard about his death on the news?" His hard tone suggested he found that omission doubtful, and he stared at her as though expecting her to flinch.

"No," Claire answered firmly, returning his unblinking stare.

"I'm visiting with everyone who has an office in this building in an effort to learn if anyone might have seen anything that would help us in our investigation. This is just an initial interview; others may follow if it proves necessary."

Claire had never seen such cold gray eyes, and their

pale contrast to his deeply tanned face was disconcerting. The captain began to pace behind Dr. Larkin's desk.

"What time did you leave the building Monday?"

"Monday?" Claire was caught off guard. Since Dr. Rhodes had been found last night, she had supposed he'd want to know when she left yesterday. She frowned, thinking. "Monday. Let's see . . . on Monday I got out of class at three twenty. I stopped at the Union for a Coke, then I came over here to my office and got ready for my Tuesday class. I guess it must have been about six thirty when I left the building."

"Did you see Dr. Rhodes before you left?"

"No. His office is on the third floor; mine's here on second, just down the hall. Directly under his as a matter of fact," she explained.

"Did you hear him moving about?"

"No. These are twelve-foot ceilings. I've never noticed any overhead noise."

"Was there anyone in the building when you left?"

"Yes. A lot of people. An evening class starts about that time, and students were beginning to gather. I believe there was also an English Club meeting that night, and kids were arriving for that. I really didn't pay much attention. I was tired and hungry and just wanted to get to my apartment."

"And after you got to your apartment, how did you spend Monday night?"

"Well," Claire began slowly, gathering her thoughts. "First I fed KayCee—"

"Casey?" His inquiry asked for an explanation.

"My cat," she explained. "Then I had supper. After I cleaned up the kitchen, I graded papers until it was time for the ten o'clock news. I watched it and then went to bed. That probably was sometime shortly before eleven."

"Did you leave your apartment at any time?"

"No. Not until the next morning. I have a nine o'clock class on Tuesdays and Thursdays."

"Can anyone corroborate that you were in your apartment all that time?"

"No. I live alone, except for my cat."

"No boyfriend?"

"No!" Claire's voice was beginning to take an edge.

"Or fiancé?" The cold gray eyes dropped to the engagement ring on her left hand.

"My fiancé is out of the country right now, working." Claire didn't like his insinuation.

"Working?"

"He's an actor. He's on location in Rome," Claire explained, pleased with the flicker of surprise her answer prompted.

"And his name is . . . ?"

"Dirk Drummond."

"Perhaps Mr. Drummond called sometime during the evening and could vouch for your presence at home."

Any response she made could be checked with a phone record, Claire knew, but she had no reason to lie.

"No, he didn't call." And he hadn't for several nights, much to her consternation.

"Did you phone anyone Monday night?" Captain Garrison continued.

Claire thought for a moment. The captain's deliberate manner made her feel that being accurate was very important. What evening was it she had called her folks in Wichita about the annual family Thanksgiving reunion they were hosting? she asked herself. Was it Monday? No. It was last night, Tuesday, she remembered, because she'd told her mother she would get there late the next afternoon and would help her make the pies, so they'd be ready for the Thursday dinner.

"No, I didn't. Not on Monday night. I did phone my parents last night, however, and I also had a call from a girlfriend."

"But Monday night you were alone, except for your cat, and neither made or received any calls," he asked for confirmation.

"That's right," Claire answered, suddenly feeling on the defensive.

"You asked if there was some special reason we wanted to see you. There is. Your name was on Dr. Rhodes' appointment calendar for ten thirty yesterday. Why?"

"Because he asked me to drop by after I got out of class. And I did, but he didn't answer the door when I knocked. I even tried it, but it was locked."

"Did you think that was odd?"

"I thought it was odd he wanted to see me."

"No, I mean did you think it was odd he didn't answer the door when you had an appointment?"

"Not really. I was late. After class some students had questions about an assignment, and I supposed something had come up that he needed to attend to."

"Why did you think it was odd he wanted to see you?"

"I couldn't imagine why he wanted to. We weren't on any committees together. He taught English lit, and I teach American lit, so we didn't have any curriculum issues. He's on the graduate faculty; I'm not, so there was nothing to discuss there. The only time he'd ever spoken to me was during my job interview and only briefly then. He hadn't spoken to me since then, not even at the cookout Dr. Larkin had for the faculty at the start of the semester. I was surprised he remembered my name."

"So when he called about the appointment, he didn't say what it was for and you didn't ask?"

"He didn't call me. He had the departmental secretary leave a note in my mailbox down in the main English office."

"I see. Maybe he wanted to discuss the problems your department is having."

Claire looked at him in quick surprise. How could he possibly know about problems in the department? She scarcely knew about them herself, and she worked here.

He noted her surprised glance. "Departmental difficulties have come up in some of my other conversations. Have the various factions approached you?"

"Off and on, and I've not been receptive. I've made it a point not to get involved."

"But you were willing to see Dr. Rhodes."

To Claire, Garrison's flat statement sounded as though her willingness to meet with the professor signaled some sinister intent on her part.

"I had no reason to refuse to see him," she explained. "I called his office shortly before noon to apologize for being late, but he didn't answer. So I left a message with the secretary saying I was sorry I'd missed him." A horrifying thought struck Claire. "Does that mean he was there, dead in his office while I was knocking on his door?" she asked aghast.

The captain looked at her closely as if judging the sincerity of her question, but his tone was neutral. "It would appear so. That's all the questions for now. We may be getting back in touch with you later. You're free to return home. Oh, there is one final question," he added as she started to turn toward the door. "Would you permit us to take a quick look around your office?"

"My office?" Claire hesitated. Her office was an embarrassing disordered mess. That was why she planned to spend part of the Thanksgiving break working on it.

"We're asking this of everyone. Of course, if you have some reason why you don't want to voluntarily give us access, it will take us a bit longer, but we can get the proper papers . . ." His voice had the edge now.

"Certainly you can look around my office." Claire resented the suggestion she had something to hide.

"Then you won't mind signing this release," the captain said as he pushed a form across the desk and handed her a pen with his left hand.

As Claire took the pen from the tanned hand she noted a pale circle around his fourth finger as though a ring had recently been removed. What a jerk; no wonder he was divorced, she thought, but she said aloud as she signed, "It's just that I hate for anyone to see my office right now. I've not had time to really get it arranged, and it's a pit." She handed the pen back. "But okay. I'll just pick up a few things and get out of your way so—"

"I'm afraid you won't be able to do that. We want to see your office as it is. The officer outside will see you from the building. Thank you for your cooperation, Dr. Markham."

And with that the cold-eyed man curtly dismissed her to the custody of a burly officer who walked her to the main door of Morrill Hall and out to the pillared porch and the wide concrete steps that lead down to Morrill Avenue. Once on the sidewalk, Claire stood a moment, glancing back up at the building. That had been unpleasant. But thank heaven it was over, and she wouldn't have to deal with that man again. Suddenly she felt the need for a cup of coffee. The closest coffee was a short block away in the Student Union, and she headed there, unaware that from Dr. Larkin's window, hard gray eyes followed her down the sidewalk.

Chapter Four

Claire frowned as she hurried down Morrill Avenue on her way to the Student Union cafeteria. As she walked, she reviewed her conversation with Captain Garrison, hoping she hadn't appeared as nervous and uneasy as she'd felt. Why had she rambled on about her surprise that Dr. Rhodes had wanted to see her? Would Garrison see something suspicious in her attempt to distance herself from the deceased professor? His close questioning regarding that unkept appointment was disturbing, and she tried to shake off her discomfort.

"If he thinks there's something suspect about having an appointment, then he ought to question someone who actually talked with Rhodes, someone like Geraldine Kosvoski or Sydney Andrews or George Karns," she muttered under her breath as she pulled open one of the heavy east doors of the redbrick Student Union.

While she had no idea why Rhodes had wanted to see her, she could guess why Geraldine and George had left his office so angrily. Both of them were coming up for tenure, and Rhodes probably had told them they wouldn't get his vote. That would be enough to upset them; Rhodes was very influential on the faculty. But the third professor, Sydney Andrews, had been given tenure last year, so why did he leave Rhodes' office looking grim? Maybe Rhodes tried to pressure him into negative votes on Geraldine and George, and they had words. That's probably it, Claire reasoned, as she walked into the food-service area of the cafeteria on her way to the tall, stainless-steel coffee dispensers. Sydney struck her as a person who would not take kindly to pressure.

Claire paid for her coffee and looked around the large seating area. The Student Union dining room was filled with people having a late breakfast, and tables were at a premium. At one nearby, three members of the English faculty were sitting, talking intently. While it was not unusual to find her colleagues visiting over coffee, Claire had never seen this particular group of three together before. Dr. Henry Millington, portly and pushing retirement, taught graduate-level English literature classes. Beside him sat Dr. David Stands, a fortysomething, sandy-haired associate professor who taught English lit survey classes and who, it was re-puted, lusted after Dr. Millington's graduate classes.

Across the table from David Stands sat one of the professors who had recently been seen leaving Rhodes' office, the tall and broad Dr. Geraldine Kosvoski. Her specialty was world literature, which seemed to include everything that wasn't written by an American or a Brit. As usual, she was dressed in drab shades of brown, a color that did nothing for her sallow complexion.

Claire thought the group an unlikely threesome. Stands wanted to take over Millington's graduate classes; Millington wasn't about to relinquish his graduate status and, like the deceased Dr. Rhodes, seemed to feel Kosvoski hadn't published enough to merit promotion and tenure; Kosvoski, of course, disagreed and was attempting to get back at Millington by supporting Stands if Stands, in turn, would support her for tenure. *Or maybe I've got that wrong,* Claire thought. *I wasn't paying very close attention when Elaine was talking about them last week.*

But whatever animosities might exist among the three, they had their heads close together now. The murder of a colleague was taking precedence over departmental conflicts. The three looked up to see Claire, with Styrofoam coffee cup in hand, searching for a place to sit. They quickly motioned her over to the empty chair at their table.

"Claire, have you talked with that Captain Garrison?" Geraldine asked.

"Yes, I just left there. He wouldn't even let me go to my office!" Claire exclaimed indignantly.

"Yeah. The same thing happened to us. We were the first ones that he interviewed," David added.

"I still can't believe Dr. Rhodes was murdered. Who would do such a thing?" Claire wondered aloud.

"I know there has been tension in the department, but nothing that would call for murder," David opined.

"Does that mean you think someone on the faculty killed Dr. Rhodes?" Geraldine asked in disbelief.

"No. I'd more likely think it was some angry student," David answered. "That's a fear we all have—that some wild-eyed, hyped-up student, furious about a grade or something, will show up with a gun. You know, like that guy at Virginia Tech."

"It wasn't a gun in this case. As I understand it, it was a letter opener," Dr. Millington interjected.

"I didn't know a letter opener could do that sort of damage," Claire exclaimed.

"Apparently. If it's been driven in hard enough," Dr. Millington answered.

"So whoever killed him would have to be really strong," Geraldine said as she tucked a strand of limp brown hair behind an ear.

For the first time, Claire noticed Geraldine's muscular arms. The woman was large-boned and solid, but not fat. The fat might come in a few years, when she rounded forty, Claire thought sympathetically. That was the reason she worked out at the Colvin Center so often.

"Either very strong or he had one heck of an adrenaline surge," David Stands noted. Then he turned to

Claire, "Dr. Larkin was looking for you. He said the police were especially eager to see you. What was that all about?"

"I guess because my name turned up on Dr. Rhodes' appointment calendar. I was supposed to see him yesterday morning, but he wasn't there."

"Oh, he was there all right; he just couldn't answer the door," Dr. Millington responded knowingly.

Geraldine Kosvoski picked up on his comment. "Yeah. Scuttlebutt has it that he was killed sometime late Monday night or very early Tuesday morning. Since he was a widower and lived alone and didn't have Tuesday or Thursday classes, no one had missed him earlier. All the police have to go on is the murder weapon."

"Hi, Sydney," David greeted a new arrival. "Did the police get through with you?" he asked as Sydney Andrews, ignoring Geraldine's dark scowl, joined the growing knot of English professors.

"Yes. I've been out awhile," he said, pulling over an empty chair from a nearby table. "Tried to work over at the library, but I couldn't keep my mind on what I was doing. This is really something, isn't it? Classes canceled and we're locked out of our offices."

"I don't understand why Garrison wants to go through our offices." Claire said between sips of coffee.

"I suppose they're looking for something incriminating, since all they have to go on is that letter opener," Sydney remarked.

"But why would the killer, assuming it's someone on

the faculty, leave anything incriminating in his own office?" Claire asked.

"Or *her* office," Sydney inserted with a nod to the world lit professor. "I'm sure Geraldine wants us to be politically correct," he added snidely.

"Andrews, you couldn't be correct, politically or any other way," Geraldine snarled, her eyes blazing.

Geraldine's bitter outburst surprised Claire. Apparently Geraldine and Sydney had a history. She noticed both Millington and Stands looked uncomfortable but not surprised. Before Syndey could reply, David quickly broke in to steer the conversation away from sensitive areas.

"I suppose it's possible the killer could have ditched something in someone else's office," he suggested.

"How could he do that?" Claire asked, eager to help David's effort to avoid a personal confrontation between Sydney and Geraldine. "We all lock our office doors. My key won't open yours; yours won't open mine. If the killer got rid of something, it would probably be in one of the restrooms."

"Not necessarily," Henry Millington answered. "The building custodian has keys. That's how William was found."

"Oh, right! A janitor killed Dr. Rhodes," Geraldine remarked sarcastically, joining the conversation.

"I didn't say that," Dr. Millington returned coolly. "I'm just suggesting it's not that difficult to get into any office."

"But how?" Claire asked. "All our keys will open is the outside door to Morrill and our own offices, no one else's. I tried to open Elaine Evan's door for her when she accidentally locked herself out, and I couldn't. She had to get Dr. Larkin to let her in."

"Right. Dr. Larkin has a master key that unlocks all the office doors." Henry Millington looked thoughtful.

"So are you saying Dr. Larkin is the murderer?" Sydney interjected.

"Right!" David answered, his sarcasm equaling that of Geraldine's. "Larkin couldn't wait two more years until Rhodes qualified for Social Security, so he decided to help him get to that big retirement party in the sky."

Millington ignored the sarcasm. "Some years ago there was another master key."

"Really? How do you know?" Geraldine asked.

"I've been here a long time. The department head before Dr. Larkin, a fellow named McMichaels, was a nice man, but he was always losing things—his wallet, his grade book, his keys. Once he couldn't even find his car out in the Morrill Hall parking lot. Anyway, every time anyone, especially the graduate teaching assistants, locked themselves out of their offices, McMichaels had to let them in, only half the time he'd misplaced his keys. Finally his secretary got tired of having to call security over and had a second master key made that she kept in her desk for those emergencies."

"Does the secretary still have that key?" Geraldine sounded as though she was on to something.

"Then could Sue Gooden be the—" Sydney began, but Dr. Millington cut him off.

"The murderer? You're certainly quick to jump to conclusions, Sydney. No, of course she isn't. But I suppose that key's still around, assuming someone hasn't taken it. However, the department has had several secretaries since then. I doubt if anyone now would even recognize that key for what it is."

"Anyone wouldn't recognize what?" asked a voice from behind Claire.

She looked around to see George Karns, the lanky blond technical writing teacher, standing behind her.

"Pull up a chair, George," Dr. Millington invited.

Millington's invitation surprised Claire. Literature professors usually treated the technical writing professors as second-class citizens, but today the department was banding together, differences temporarily forgotten. Tomorrow they would realize they had a new reason for being suspicious of one another, Claire thought. One of their number might well be a murderer.

"I'd have been over here sooner," Karns said, "but I was no more than out the door of Morrill when some reporter from Channel Four stuck a mike in my face and started asking me questions. I know less about Rhodes' death than the reporter did."

While the men discussed ambush interviews and stabbed literature professors, Geraldine leaned toward Claire and said softly, "I'm surprised Sydney wondered if Sue did it. They were dating earlier this fall. Maybe he knows something about sweet little Sue that the rest of us don't."

"They were dating?" The two seemed like an unlikely couple to Claire.

"For a little while. That snake always hits on new secretaries. And single faculty women too, so watch it. I speak from experience," she said with a sideways glare at Sydney that suggested the parting had not been pleasant.

Ah, that explains it, Claire thought, remembering the woman's earlier angry outburst.

"Thanks for the warning; I—"

"Ah, Dr. Markham, I've been looking for you. Captain Garrison wants to see you. He says it's urgent."

Claire twisted in her chair at the sound of Dr. Larkin's voice. The balding department head had just walked in behind her.

"I've already been interviewed, sir," she replied, looking up into Larkin's strained face and worried eyes. *No wonder he's upset*, she thought. A *murdered faculty member is enough to upset any department head*. In fact, everyone was feeling the tension, she realized. That was why the clever banter and the one-upsman repartee that usually sprinkled the conversation when the faculty got together was missing today.

"Yes, I know, but he wants to see you again. He asked me to locate you."

Dr. Larkin sounded concerned, but he didn't sound as concerned as Claire suddenly felt.

Chapter Five

Claire felt as though she were twelve and had just been hauled into the principal's office. She stood before Dr. Larkin's desk in the spot where she had already been questioned earlier that morning. And the cold-eyed captain still confronted her across the desk as he had before. But this time his face and voice were as cold as his eyes.

"Have you seen this before?" he asked, motioning to the large brown briefcase sitting on the desk.

Claire eyed the leather case. It looked like what every third professor on campus carried.

"That briefcase? I don't know. A lot of professors carry them. I might have seen someone with it. I couldn't say."

"So it's not yours."

"No."

"Then can you tell me how it happened to be in your office?" Garrison's voice was as coldly crisp and hard as freshly cracked ice. And that cracked ice sent a sudden shiver racing down Claire's spine.

"In my office? That briefcase wasn't in my office," Claire protested.

"Officer Kendell here"—the captain nodded in the direction of the blond-headed uniformed campus policeman who stood at the side of the room—"found it hidden behind the logs of the fireplace in your office, despite the chairs that were obscuring it."

Claire frowned, confused. Was he suggesting she had purposely arranged the chairs that way in order to mask the fireplace from view because she had hidden the briefcase there?

"To answer your question, that briefcase must have been left by the person who had that office before me."

"Was that person's initials W.A.R.?"

"No, I don't think so."

"I didn't think so, either. Dr. William Rhodes' middle name was Allen. The briefcase belonged to him." And he turned the case so she could see the initials in gold by the clasp: W.A.R.

"But then why was it in my—"

"Exactly, Dr. Markham," the icy voice cut in. "That's what we're trying to determine."

"If I were hiding something that belonged to Dr. Rhodes, why would I have given you permission to search my office?" Claire asked in an attempt to establish her innocence.

"As I recall our earlier conversation, you intended to get there before we did. Perhaps there was something you hoped to take with you." He cast a knowing glance at the brown briefcase.

"Yes!" Claire exclaimed, beginning to bristle. "There was something I wanted to take with me! A test I'm working on. Since classes were dismissed today, I was going to use the time to finish it."

"Perhaps." The frigid gray eyes bore into hers as though, once more, he expected her to flinch. She wouldn't give him the satisfaction and stared straight back.

"Did you lock your office door when you left the building Monday evening?"

"Yes. I always lock the door when I leave the office."

"Then how could a briefcase be left in your office if the door was locked?'

"I wouldn't know—unless—" She paused, remembering. "Dr. Larkin has a master key. He can get into any office in the English department."

"Are you suggesting Dr. Larkin put this briefcase in your office?" he asked, unable to keep the disbelief from his voice.

"Of course not, but someone else must have. I'm just saying I'm not the only one who can unlock my office."

"I see. So you're implying some person might have stolen the key from Dr. Larkin?"

"It's possible, I suppose."

"His master key hasn't been stolen. We've been using it to get in to check the offices."

"But doesn't security have master keys to all the buildings too? And for that matter, the night custodians have master keys. Maybe one of them had theirs stolen," Claire suggested.

"All of those keys have been accounted for."

Captain Garrison's icy stare was making Claire more and more uncomfortable. That briefcase was forming a silent and sinister connection between herself and Dr. Rhodes' death. The captain, apparently working faster than she thought possible, had anticipated the ways her office might have been unlocked and had checked them out. But there was one way he wasn't aware of, she realized, recalling the conversation in the Student Union.

"Several of us were talking about this over in the Union just now, and some years ago a departmental secretary had a second master key made because the department head at that time kept misplacing the one he had."

"Who told you that?"

"Dr. Millington. Like I said, a group of us were visiting in the Union about—about what happened. That's where Dr. Larkin found me and said you wanted to see me again."

"Did Dr. Millington also say what had happened to the second master key?"

"No. He just supposed over the years it was mislaid and lost."

"So Sue Gooden—that's the secretary's name, isn't it?" he asked of the young officer for confirmation, who nodded in agreement. "So Ms. Gooden had a second master key made—"

This time it was Claire's turn to interrupt. "No, it wasn't Sue. Dr. Millington said it was some former secretary—apparently the department has gone though a number of them."

"I understand you were involved in a murder case earlier this year."

The quick shift in topic surprised Claire, and the sudden memory of the heavy fireplace poker swinging down on her head caused her to blanch.

"Yes," she whispered hoarsely.

"Interesting. And here you are involved in another murder case."

"But I was the intended victim, not the murderer. Besides, I think the charge was manslaughter, not murder," she protested, regaining her composure.

The nearby officer quickly looked though a sheaf of papers in his hands and murmured quietly, "She's right, Captain, on both points."

Claire thought the captain looked disappointed.

"And you still insist you have no notion why Dr. Rhodes wanted to see you Tuesday?"

"I have no idea what he wanted to talk about," Claire said, returning his frigid stare.

"Might it have something to do with this?" And he pulled from the briefcase a copy of her book, her published dissertation. "A book about an American children's author strikes me as a rather odd book for a professor of Elizabethan and Jacobean literature to be carrying around."

Once more Claire was caught off guard. Why would Dr. Rhodes be interested in a children's writer? She groped for an answer. "Maybe he wanted me to—"

"Autograph it for him?" Garrison finished for her sarcastically.

Claire frowned at the rude, uncalled-for remark. He was discrediting what she said before she said it, and he wouldn't do that unless he was convinced he'd found the killer. Claire stared at the hard face. She had been right. He was a jerk, and worse, he was a jerk who made rapid and erroneous judgments—not a good trait in a homicide investigator. Perhaps he realized the crudeness of his comment. But his quick look of discomfort disappeared as rapidly as it had come.

"You were saying . . ." he said, inviting her to finish.

"I was going to say maybe he wanted me to explain something in my analysis of the stories. I demonstrated that the published work was not Professor Comfort's, as everyone's believed for years, but his sister's. Maybe there was something Dr. Rhodes didn't agree with. He'd done a similar study years ago when he built a case for why Francis Bacon couldn't have written Shakespeare's plays, and maybe he . . ." Claire forced herself to stop. Nervousness was threatening to make her ramble again. Garrison probably read nervousness as guilt.

The captain returned the book to the briefcase. "So what do we have here, Dr. Markham? A mysterious appointment scheduled with the murdered man. The briefcase belonging to that man hidden in your office. An office you say was locked. In that hidden briefcase among other papers is a copy of a book you have written. And you cannot prove you didn't leave your apartment the night of the murder."

Claire didn't respond. She didn't like the way this interview was going. A knot began to twist in her stomach.

"Tell me, how long have you been doing weight training?" he asked suddenly.

Once more Claire was jarred by his unexpected shift in direction.

"Weight training! How on earth could you know—"

"You're not the only one who works out at the Colvin Center. I've seen you there on the machines."

And although she had never noticed him, the captain could easily have seen her at the center. She worked out there almost daily. Anyone engaged to a rising Hollywood leading man needed to keep in shape if she had half a brain.

"You appear to be a strong woman."

"Are you suggesting I'm strong enough to drive a letter opener into someone's neck?"

"Are you?"

"I wouldn't know. I've never tried. Look, Captain Garrison. Should I be hiring a lawyer?"

"Do you feel you need one?"

"I feel like you're trying to set me up," she answered defensively.

"I'm trying to find a murderer."

"So, in your mind, I'm the best candidate? Let's see. Apart from having Dr. Rhodes' briefcase, I had means. The letter opener, I suppose, was lying there on his desk waiting to be used, and you think I have enough muscle to shove it into his neck. I had opportunity, because I can't prove I didn't leave my apartment Monday night. But what was my motive? Why on earth would I want Dr. Rhodes dead? I didn't even know the man!"

"I'm working on that. And for the time being you are not to leave Stillwater."

"I can't leave town?" she asked in disbelief.

"No."

"But tomorrow is Thanksgiving. My parents are expecting me."

"Do they live in Stillwater?"

"No. In Wichita."

"Then in that case you'd better plan to have your Thanksgiving dinner here in town."

"You mean I can't even go to my folks' for the holiday?" she asked, unwilling to accept what she was hearing.

"Maybe they can bring the turkey down here," he answered in a tone that fell just short of sarcasm.

"Not with a houseful of relatives arriving. Am I under arrest?"

"Not yet. Right now you're just 'a person of interest'

in the investigation. But don't try to leave town. That's all for now, Dr. Markham. If you want to pick up that test, the officer here will accompany you to your office."

Claire's green eyes blazed at the insolent captain, who was satisfied he had found the murderer. He didn't trust her to go to her own office! He was sending someone with her, apparently to make sure she didn't make off with any more of Dr. Rhodes' possessions. Furious, she turned on her heel and strode from the room. The young officer had to trot to catch up with her. But as angry as she was, she was even more frightened.

Claire's fear would have increased had she known her escorted progress to her office was being observed with intense interest. A figure in a brown jacket stood at the west end of the long hallway and watched as she disappeared into her office followed by the officer.

So they're letting her back in. If only I could have gotten there before the police did! They must have found Rhodes' briefcase. That has to be why Garrison pulled her back in a second time. If the briefcase has been found, so be it. Nothing can be done about that. And maybe Rhodes wasn't carrying what I want—what I need. I didn't check. Should have, but couldn't. But those things weren't in his office, so that case is the only other place they could be, unless he'd left them at his house. His house. That's a thought.

The dark eyes glittered once more and the cruel mouth pulled into a nasty grin as the clever mind behind those glittering eyes began playing with an idea—an idea with real possibilities.

But wherever they are, the police found his briefcase in her locked office. An obvious conclusion would be that she had taken and hidden it. And she couldn't have gotten the briefcase if she hadn't been in Rhodes' office. Being there, she could have grabbed that letter opener just as I did. According to her buddy Elaine, she was at home all Monday night alone. Okay. She had access to the weapon and the opportunity to use it. But why would she have been in Rhodes' office? What would have been her motive?

The figure in the brown jacket frowned at that thought.

There has to be some compelling reason for killing Rhodes. Not denial of tenure, probably. She hasn't been here long enough for that to be a pressing concern. It has to be something else. All I have to do is come up with it and leak it to Garrison. Then Claire Markham takes the rap, and I'm home free.

The figure smiled at the prospect of shifting the onus to Claire.

But first there's the problem of a motive. Rhodes always went after people on the basis of their scholarship. All I know she's written is that book about that kids' author. I wonder if Rhodes had read it. Probably, knowing him. What if he'd found something suspect in it . . .

shoddy scholarship or plagiarism. That's a thought! Plagiarism!

The smile grew into a wide grin at the delicious irony. The figure turned and started down the west stairs. The glittering eyes were evidence of a mind busily at work.

Chapter Six

Claire, hampered by an armload of books and papers, bumped her apartment door closed with her hip, dumped her things on the desk, and reached for the city phone directory. KayCee, her calico cat, looked up disdainfully from her interrupted nap and meowed in annoyance, but her feline displeasure went unnoticed. Claire was focused on the directory's yellow pages under the heading "Attorneys."

Captain Garrison apparently thought his murder case was going to be solved quickly at her expense. The knot in her stomach told her she needed a lawyer. But as she scanned the list of fifty-eight names, she groaned in dismay. She was new to Stillwater and was unacquainted with any lawyers either by name or reputation. So on what basis could she make a good decision about who to hire should she need legal counsel? The directory advertisements suggested the local lawyers were more skilled in personal injury and divorce cases than in criminal cases. Her mind raced. Who did she know who might be able to advise her? The only person she could think of was Jack Evans, Elaine's husband. He was a computer consultant who worked out of his home. If she was lucky, perhaps she could catch him there, and she dialed the Evans residence.

Elaine, home early due to canceled classes, already had filled Jack in on what had been discovered in Dr. Rhodes' office, so Claire didn't have to go into all the details, and she concentrated on why she felt she needed to see a lawyer. Fortunately Jack could help her. He'd had occasion to see Jacob Prior in action when the attorney had defended a former client of his, and Jack endorsed him. Claire quickly phoned the law office of Prior and Prior. Jacob Prior wasn't available. He was in court in Oklahoma City, and tomorrow was a holiday, so an appointment was scheduled for early Friday afternoon. The knot in her stomach loosened slightly.

Next she needed to call her parents before they began to wonder why she hadn't arrived. It was a call she wouldn't have had to make had she left for Wichita immediately after Garrison dismissed her the first time, she thought ruefully. Instead, she had gone to the Union for coffee only to be summoned back before the accusing officer. The call was difficult to make. How could she tell her parents she was a murder suspect in a way that wouldn't worry them and ruin the annual family Thanksgiving reunion? How could she put a positive face on her situation when what she really wanted was to feel her father's strong arm around her shoulders and see her mother's smile of fierce protective love. When she called, Claire attempted to softened the situation a bit by implying that since the investigation was just beginning, all the faculty were being asked to stay in town for a few days.

But that was not the end of Claire's anxieties. The entire day seemed to conspire against her. As if she didn't have enough to make her angry and frightened, quite by accident that evening she blundered onto another cause of anxiety. While she was eating a supper of tomato soup and crackers, she idly flipped though the television channels trying to find something to take her mind off Captain Garrison's suspicions. She had just hit *Access Hollywood* when her finger stopped on the remote's channel-advance button. To her complete surprise, her fiancé's handsome face filled the screen. Claire almost spilled her soup in her haste to punch up the volume. This was Dirk's first appearance on the program, and he hadn't told her to watch for it.

Claire had missed the setup for the piece, but apparently the thrust of the segment was how the casts and crews of three separate movies on location in Rome were planning to spend the American Thanksgiving holiday so far from home. The camera pulled back from a close-up of Dirk to show the entire group of nine actors who were currently working on films ranging from a madcap comic romp through the Italian capital to Dirk's action-suspense film to a historical romance set in de' Medici Italy. Claire's smile of happy surprise quickly faded into a grimace of concern. Her fiancé was bracketed on either side by two stunning women, one blond and one brunette. The jolt she felt was not totally unexpected. She had known for months this sort of thing would happen, but being forewarned didn't soften the blow that forced the air from her lungs, making her gasp.

"But you might as well get used to it," she said aloud, pushing down a surge of anger and fear. "If Dirk decides to remain a professional actor, that goes with the territory, so don't let it bother you. Don't turn into an insecure, whining twit. If you can't trust him, you better not marry him." But following her own advice was hard. Those women were beautiful and were in Rome with him. She was in Oklahoma without him.

Claire's attention focused on the attractive brunette, who was sitting very close to Dirk and leaning in his direction. Claire didn't know much about body language, but she could read those signals plainly enough. Anyone could. The interviewer had just turned to the dark beauty, the female star of the historical romance, who had arrived for the session in period costume, her ample bosom threatening to spill out of the low-cut bodice.

"Speaking of 'historical romance,'" the interviewer

said with a suggestive lilt to her voice, "I understand that you and Dirk here have a little romantic history. What's is like to get back together with this good-looking guy, Jill?"

Jill! Claire knew the name! The sensuous brunette with the burgeoning bustline was Jill Tyler, the actress Dirk had been engaged to, the girl who broke up with him when he chose to take a teaching job at a small Kansas college. She was in Rome? With him! And Dirk hadn't mentioned it!

"It's been wonderful catching up with each other again. I'm so glad Dirk's decided to resume his career," she answered in a husky, sultry voice as she looked up at Dirk through a veil of heavy lashes.

Claire missed Dirk's polite and gallant response. She was too busy with a profane response of her own, her good intentions forgotten.

"And what else has he decided to resume?" Claire hotly asked the dark beauty on the TV screen. "Has he resumed things with you too?" Was Jill the reason he hadn't called?

This time she could not beat back her anger and fear. Claire pushed her bowl of tomato soup aside, stalked to her desk, and punched on her computer. As soon as it booted up, she went online and typed in Dirk's e-mail address.

Why didn't you tell me Jill's in Rome? Did you think I wouldn't find out you've been seeing her?

She shoved the cursor to Send, but before she clicked the mouse, she read the irate message. She paused. She read it a second time. Then instead of clicking Send, Claire pressed the Delete key. *Calm down*, she cautioned herself. *Don't send anything in anger. Don't back him into a corner. Give him an opening and see what he does with it.* Taking a deep breath, she typed a new message.

> *Hi, Hon. Saw you being interviewed tonight on TV. Glad you're being noticed. I won't be going to the folks' for Thanksgiving tomorrow. I'm under suspicion of murder. Love you. Claire*

She read the message a second time and smiled grimly. If that didn't get a response, nothing would. With a click of her mouse, the message was on its way.

At 3:30 in the morning, Claire was jarred into consciousness by a ringing phone. The caller was a frantic Dirk.

"Claire! What are you talking about?! Who was murdered? Why are you a suspect?"

"What? Dirk? Is that you?" Claire asked trying to wake up.

"Yes, it's me. I know it's early there, but I waited as long as I could before calling. Claire, that's happened? What are you talking about?"

An hour later Claire hung up, smiling. She had told him everything she knew regarding the murder of Dr.

William Rhodes and why she was "a person of interest." And without having to ask him directly, Claire learned Jill's recent arrival in Rome had caught Dirk by surprise, and they had chatted only briefly before the *Access Hollywood* segment had been taped. Claire hoped her relief hadn't been apparent when Dirk told her that he and the whole crew were leaving that afternoon for location shots in Venice.

She was still smiling when she returned to bed, secure in the knowledge that she was missed and loved. Sleep came far more easily than it had when she had first gone to bed, tormented with thoughts of Garrison's suspicions and Dirk's possible infidelity. Although it was early, today was Thanksgiving, and Claire knew she had something to be truly thankful for: Dirk Drummond loved and needed her just as she loved and needed him.

Chapter Seven

When she awoke for the second time that morning, Claire discovered Thanksgiving Day had dawned bright and sunny. While the days and certainly the nights could be windy and cold, Stillwater had yet to receive its first snow, which, according to the locals, often didn't arrive until the first of the year. In fact, many of the trees still had their foliage. While the boughs of the maples and sweetgums were bare, the oaks and Bradford pears kept most of their leaves, which had turned russet and deep red. The broad, glossy leaves of the magnolias, evergreen in this climate, shone vividly verdant in the morning sun.

It was a glorious fall day in central Oklahoma. But Claire wasn't able to appreciate neither the weather nor the trees. The warm, safe feelings of love and protection kindled earlier during her conversation with Dirk weakened in the bright light of morning. She was alone and she was worried. Dirk might love her, but she had never been a murder suspect before. Troubled by Captain Garrison's suspicions, angry she couldn't leave town, and hungry because her refrigerator was empty in anticipation of the holiday spent at her parents, she remembered a cafeteria ad she had seen in the Stillwater *NewsPress*. At noon, looking trim in a dark green pantsuit and flats, she left for her first restaurant Thanksgiving dinner.

As she paid the cashier and picked up her tray, Claire realized she should have gotten to the cafeteria earlier. Of course, the Sirloin Steak House was packed that day. It was Thanksgiving, and apparently half of Stillwater was having its turkey dinner out. She glanced at her tray: turkey, mashed potatoes, gravy, green beans, yams, cranberry salad, and pumpkin pie. That's what she should be eating at her folks' house today. Instead, her worried parents were trying to explain to the relatives why she wasn't joining them. And she wasn't joining them because the Oklahoma State University police force, at the direction of Captain Garrison, wouldn't allow her to leave town. So now she was trying to find a place to sit in the crowded restaurant that offered a "Full Thanksgiving Dinner for Only $9.99 Plus Tax."

Claire slowly walked the aisles. All the tables were full, and the food on her tray was beginning to cool. In desperation she started looking for people who were eating dessert. She'd stand nearby and grab a chair as soon as it was vacated. But no one seemed to be ready for their pie just yet. The gravy on her mashed potatoes was beginning to congeal when she heard a voice behind her.

"You're welcome to share my table if you like."

A gentleman! Claire turned toward the voice, smiling.

"Thank you, if you really don't mind, I'd—" Both her voice and her smile died in midsentence. The man who had risen and was indicating the empty chair opposite him was the last person on earth she wanted to share a table with. The offer had come from Captain Grant Garrison, who was sitting alone at a table for two.

"Captain Garrison! What are you doing here?" Claire made no attempt to hide her surprised disapproval.

"Even a policeman gets to have Thanksgiving dinner. And since I'm the reason you're spending the holiday in town, the least I can do is share my table with you."

Claire's back stiffened and her green eyes hardened. "No, thank you. I'd rather wait." Her voice fairly crackled with contempt, a tone that was overheard by the diners at the next table, and the family of four looked up warily at the two facing each other.

"You'd rather wait than sit with me? I thought you might feel that way, but you're blocking the aisle and people are beginning to stare," he said softly. "Why don't you sit down."

Realizing she was on the verge of making a scene and with no place else to sit, Claire fought back her anger and thumped her tray down on the small table. Captain Garrison waited until she was seated before he sat and spoke again.

"Actually, I'm glad to see you. I've been wanting to apologize."

"Apologize?"

"For the heavy-handed way I interviewed you. I'm sorry I came on so strong. But, truth be told, after many years in law enforcement this is my first murder investigation. Please mark my ineptness up to inexperience. Maybe I should let the Oklahoma State Bureau of Investigation take over. They certainly want to," he added sharply.

But he didn't look or sound as though he was willing to give way to the OSBI. That agency probably was eager to handle the murder case that had occurred on state property, Claire thought.

"I'm surprised the OSBI doesn't have the case, or, if not them, the Stillwater police," she said, giving voice to her thought.

"The OSU police force is fully licensed by the state, and the murder occurred in our jurisdiction. Did you think we were just some night watchman operation?" the captain asked defensively.

The suggestion his force was somehow inferior seemed to rankle Captain Garrison, and Claire was secretly pleased she had hit a nerve. Turnabout was fair play. His suspicion had certainly unnerved her.

"Just so you know, I'm seeing a lawyer tomorrow.

And just so *I'll* know, have you come up with a motive for me yet?"

"No. Not yet."

"But you're looking?"

"I have to look at everything."

Although she disliked sitting at his table, Claire realized doing so gave her an opportunity to argue her case. Maybe she could get him to look somewhere other than at her.

"If I had taken that briefcase, why on earth would I have stuffed it in the fireplace when I could have locked it in my file cabinet? It wouldn't have been in view that way."

"Well, there is that," Captain Garrison admitted. "And it does seem if you had taken Rhodes' briefcase, it wouldn't have still been in your office. You would have had all day Tuesday to get rid of it."

"Then why am I having Thanksgiving dinner here instead of in Wichita?" Claire demanded.

"Because you still had means and opportunity. You're still 'a person of interest.' But I am following up on your idea of the second master key."

Claire didn't respond. If that comment was supposed to make her feel better, it didn't. She concentrated on her turkey. The sooner she ate, the sooner she could leave. She would sit at his table, but she didn't have to talk with him. She kept her eyes on her plate, refusing to glance up at the man, even when she was sure he was looking at her.

And he was looking at her. She was very easy to look at. The sunlight streaming through the wide plate-glass window made red-and-gold highlights dance in her heavy, shoulder-length chestnut hair. A tiny pulse beat in her throat as she quickly and neatly ate the meal before her. Occasionally her short, straight nose flared— *probably with dislike of me,* he thought. Those startling green eyes were hidden behind a dark screen of lowered lashes. Claire was reaching for her pumpkin pie when he broke the silence.

"I'm reading your book."

"Really?" She was so surprised she looked up at him despite herself. There was a flash of appreciation in the green eyes that had been focused on her plate.

Her quick look of pleasure caused him to feel a little stab of guilt. She was plainly pleased he had been interested in her work. And he was. He'd started reading her book, an exposé of the children's author Coe Z. Comfort, last night, before he found that note under his door this morning. The message, constructed of letters clipped from a magazine and glued on a piece of computer paper, was brief: *Garrison, check Markham's book. Rhodes did.*

"I'm finding it very interesting. You must like playing detective."

"It had its satisfying moments." Then she added, almost to herself, "And some moments that weren't so satisfying."

"Like what happened after that professor Wilfred

Purdy lost his job because you proved he'd deliberately destroyed evidence that contradicted his glowing biography of Comfort?"

"Yes. How did you know? Losing his job wasn't in my book. That happened later."

"I read the report the Winfield police faxed down here. So, this Purdy person went after you with a fireplace poker just because he'd lost his job?" The captain sounded as though he found that difficult to believe.

"It was more than just losing that job; he had lost any chance of ever teaching at a reputable college or university. He was ruined professionally. Consequently, he intended to 'ruin' me anyway he could, and the quickest way was with a fireplace poker."

"So being ruined professionally drove him to murder," Garrison said thoughtfully. "That might be the motive in the Rhodes' case."

"Maybe, but it's not a motive you can lay to me. If Dr. Rhodes was trying to hurt me professionally, I wasn't aware of it. Besides, wouldn't robbery or maybe vengeance by an irate student be more likely motives?" Claire asked, eager to put as much distance as possible between herself and a reason for Rhodes' death.

"They're the more obvious ones." Aware he might be saying too much to a prime suspect, Garrison continued anyway. "But Dr. Rhodes was wearing an expensive watch and his wallet was in his jacket pocket when his body was found. It appears that only his briefcase was taken. An irate student? That could be, I suppose. That's what the OSBI wants to push."

Claire noticed his slight frown and the narrowing of his lips at the mention of the OSBI. Apparently Captain Garrison chaffed at that agency's attempts to take over. Claire knew Garrison could be an arrogant man. And he must be a proud man too. Claire realized that apologizing to her had been difficult for him, but he had done it. And she would be as rude as he had been if she didn't acknowledge his effort.

"I do appreciate your apology about that interview. Thank you—even if you still think I'm a murderer. And thank you for sharing your table." She slipped her purse strap over her shoulder and, with a nod, quickly left the table before he could rise.

As the slim young woman walked away, the captain whispered softly, "Yes. You're still a person of interest." And the gray eyes that watched her leave the restaurant were no longer cold or distant.

Chapter Eight

Late Friday night the Oklahoma City media covering Rhodes' murder received an anonymous tip regarding the location of the slain professor's missing briefcase, and the word spread rapidly. By early Saturday morning both Claire's phone and doorbell began to ring with reporters from around the state seeking interviews, which Claire steadfastly refused to grant. They persisted with tape recorders and camcorders at the ready, hoping to waylay her if she left the building and goad her into a response to their shouted questions. Claire, heeding her own inclination as well as her lawyer's advice, stayed indoors with her phone disconnected and shades drawn. Finally by midafternoon, with deadlines for the Sunday morning editions looming, the reporters left in search of more forthcoming sources. As she watched them leave, Claire wondered what sorts of questions she'd face on campus when classes started again.

The Monday after Thanksgiving break, the faculty were allowed back into their offices, and English classes resumed. Dr. Rhodes had been dead a week, and no arrests had yet been made. The investigation was moving slowly. When Claire stopped by the main office on her way in, Sue Gooden was sorting mail and telling the part-time secretary what had happened Friday.

"Yeah, even though it was a holiday, the police had me and Dr. Larkin back up here Friday morning. That Captain Garrison—now he's one good-looking guy— asked me about another master key he claimed there was. No one ever told me about an extra master key. I told him I've never seen one, but he was welcome to look all he wanted. They went through everything, but they didn't find any such key. Dr. Larkin didn't know anything about a second master key either. Then the police asked him who had been the secretary before me." The redheaded young woman glanced up from the mail in her hand when she turned and saw Claire. Her friendly, chatty tone changed to abrupt, almost snippy, and her freckled turned-up nose turned up even farther. "Oh, hello, Dr. Markham. I'll have this mail sorted in a minute."

"No hurry. I'll get it later," Claire answered pleasantly,

turning back to the door. As she left the office so did Sue's scarcely disguised ill humor, and she heard the secretary continue her gossip.

"I don't think those OSBI lab people are ever going to get finished with Dr. Rhodes' office. There's still yellow tape across his door," Claire heard Sue say.

Apparently Garrison was having to rely on outside help whether he wanted to or not, Claire thought as she walked down the hall, and that notion perversely pleased her. She was also pleased that Garrison had been unable to find the master key. A missing master key meant someone else might have it, someone who could have opened her office. Unless . . . unless . . . Her smile of pleasure faded at a disturbing thought. Unless Henry Millington was wrong about there ever having been a second key.

Uneasy at the thought the aging professor might be mistaken and that her students might have heard she was "a person of interest" in the murder investigation, Claire was uncomfortable returning to the classroom. Already many of the faculty were giving her strange, speculative looks. She was no more than through the door of her 9:30 American lit survey class than she was accosted by Gary Morris, a pudgy, talkative student.

"Dr. Markham, is it true the police are talking to every student that Dr. Rhodes ever had?" he asked eagerly.

Apparently Captain Garrison was bowing to OSBI pressure to check on students, and it probably was a good idea, Claire thought as she laid her notes on the lectern before unwinding the long scarf around her neck and slipping out of her jacket.

"Gary, I doubt if *every* student Dr. Rhodes *ever* had could be found, let alone be interviewed, but the police might want to talk with any student who had recently failed one of his courses, I suppose."

The hefty jock who was taking Survey of American Lit as a humanities credit joined the conversation.

"I heard they arrested the department secretary, and she's in jail."

"Really?" Claire was surprised. Apparently a conversation and a desk search were enough for the rumor mill to label a person a murderer. With an inward grimace, she wondered what sorts of stories were being circulated about her.

"Yeah, on Friday," the football guard added.

"Well, she was in the main office sorting mail when I arrived this morning, and she didn't mention being arrested," Claire answered. "How do stories like that get started?"

"I heard that guy who got killed was found with a butcher knife in his back," a slender blonde on the front row eagerly interjected.

"No. I heard his throat was cut!" Another student cut in excitedly.

His throat wasn't cut, but you're getting warmer, Claire thought, but she said, "That sounds like another rumor to me. However, class, it's not a rumor that there will be a test on Friday as promised."

The reminder of the upcoming exam was greeted with a chorus of groans as the class settled into their desks and Claire opened her lecture notes.

As soon as she returned to her office after class, Claire had company. Geraldine Kosvoski, with coffee mug in hand, stood in her doorway. The world lit prof was a drab study in unattractive shades of brown from her limp, mousey brown hair to her scuffed brown loafers. Personal enhancement was obviously not a high priority with Geraldine Kosvoski.

"The police have started interviewing students," she announced.

"Have they? Any likely candidates?" Claire asked. Apparently her student Gary was partially right; at least some students were being interviewed. Captain Garrison, desperate for leads, was following the urging of the OSBI.

Geraldine set her coffee mug down long enough to move a box of books from a chair and to sit down.

"Good grief, Claire. When are you going to put this stuff away?" she groused good-naturedly before continuing. "Rhodes was a tough grader," she said, dropping into the chair she had cleared, "and he's failed more than one student. However, there is one obvious contender. A big guy named Leon Creedmore; he's currently working on a masters. A real hothead."

"A hothead?"

"Yeah, he has a bad temper, plus he's one of those students who feel the rules don't apply to him. He's always looking for an edge, trying to get some requirement waived, and he's a real argumentative pain in class. Everyone who teaches a grad class hopes he won't show up in theirs."

"Had Dr. Rhodes failed him?"

"Not yet, but apparently things were headed that way. He was in Rhodes' office last Monday morning arguing. Before he left, he could be heard yelling that he was married and had a baby and couldn't waste time retaking a class. So maybe he came back later in the day or found Rhodes up here working that night."

"I suppose that's possible," Claire agreed, discomforted to think a student might resort to that extreme, but at the same time, she was relieved someone had a better motive for murder than she.

That afternoon Claire was still getting strange stares from people on campus, but by Tuesday when she hadn't been arrested yet, curiosity began to wane. And by Wednesday, her students, at least, were more interested in the start of basketball season than they were with a murdered English professor.

Wednesday was also the day of Dr. Rhodes' funeral, which had been delayed for the arrival of his sons from Chicago and Atlanta. The service was held late that afternoon in Stillwater's First Presbyterian Church. In addition to friends and acquaintances from the campus and town and the entire English faculty, the university president along with the deans of the seven colleges sat in one formidable group in the front left of the sanctuary. Claire, almost late, slipped into the last pew. She had dismissed her afternoon class early in order to make the ceremony.

From her seat at the rear of the sanctuary, Claire noticed by the way the faculty seated themselves that the camaraderie, which had existed among the professors since Dr. Rhodes' death, was beginning to dissolve into its former factions. The literature faculty sat midway down the center section while the technical writing professors gathered across the aisle. And even in the center section, the graduate and senior faculty were a bit removed from those who taught lower-division literature classes. And within the latter group, those without tenure seemed to cluster together. The graduate teaching assistants who staffed most of the sections of Freshman Composition sat together in the rear on the north side of the sanctuary. Claire decided that while she would join no faction, she would pay more attention to the issues and personnel involved. She had no motive for killing Dr. Rhodes, but someone else had, and that someone might well be here at the funeral. The campus police seemed to be paying attention to those conflicts too. Although she was still "a person of interest" and confined to the city limits, Claire was relieved she was no longer the only person of interest.

The organ was playing softly as Dr. Rhodes' two sons and their families were escorted to the center front of the sanctuary. The Rhodes sons, both in dark suits, appeared to be men on the cusp of forty. They shared a family resemblance: medium height, fair thinning hair, and prominent noses. They had the look and bearing of men who led responsible, sedentary lives behind desks. Their wives, conservatively dressed and neatly coiffured, while not trophy wives, were attractive enough for their ages. Both couples had two children. Dr. Rhodes' four grandchildren appeared to range in age from nine to fourteen.

The somber group had just been seated when another person strode down the aisle to join the Rhodes family. The late arrival was tall, taller than Dirk, Claire noted, and broader across the shoulders and chest too. His dark hair was close-cropped, and in physique and coloring he looked nothing like his brothers. Claire wondered if he might be another brother; he certainly had the family nose, although given his size, his fit his face better than the noses of his brothers fit theirs. But if he was a brother, the family must not have been very close because his arrival seemed to be unexpected. It appeared to startle the rest of the Rhodes family; however, the men rose quickly to shake his hand, the wives nodded in greeting, and the children stared at the newcomer in wonder. Unlike his suited siblings, he wrote a dark sweater, sport coat, and slacks. The man's manner seemed as casual as his dress. He grinned at his nephews and winked at his nieces. Stern looks from their fathers stifled the children's giggles. Claire couldn't be sure, sitting at the rear of the church as she was, but the wives appeared to be exchanging sly smiles with the late arrival as the organ finished the final chord of the prelude and the minister took his place behind the pulpit.

At that moment someone slid into the pew directly across the aisle from Claire, and she glanced over to see that the latecomer was Captain Garrison. She looked away quickly. What was he doing here? Checking who among the twenty-two English faculty members didn't show up? Claire stole a look from the corner of her eye. She was right. He seemed to be taking roll, noticing who was sitting with whom as she had done. Was he also going to note who cried and who didn't? If tears were to be taken as a sign of innocence, she was in trouble. She hadn't known Dr. Rhodes, and she couldn't cry for someone she didn't know. In fact, she had a difficult time keeping her mind on the eulogy. In the warm church listening to the well-modulated monotone of the minister, Claire's attention wandered as she retraced the events of the past week.

Explaining to her parents why she couldn't join them for the Thanksgiving dinner family reunion had been difficult. They had been shocked to learn of the departmental death and upset that their daughter was one of those under suspicion. The next day they had driven down to see her and the attorney she had retained.

However, not all had been difficult. Her long distance calls to Dirk in Italy were more lengthy and more personal than they had been for some time. Their relationship had been strained. Their wedding had been put on hold. Dirk had the opportunity to play the second lead in the action-suspense movie being shot in Italy. Consequently, he'd taken a semester's leave of absence from the private college where he had been teaching in order to accept the role. Claire had been offered a teaching position at the same small college, but with Dirk gone for a semester, very possibly not to return to college teaching, she had accepted a job at Oklahoma State University at almost twice what the private college was able to pay her. Although neither of them had said so in so many words, both harbored the notion they had been run out on by the other. But with Claire's current difficulty, their calls were frequent and intimate. Dirk was frustrated he couldn't be with her, and Claire was grateful for his deep concern. She smiled remembering their conversation last night. Wow! Hearing him express his feelings so graphically almost made it worth being accused of murder.

And the thought of being accused of murder caused her to glance once more across the aisle at the man who considered her a possible suspect. He was looking at her, and the smile that thoughts of Dirk had generated quickly disappeared from her lips.

Not good, Claire! she admonished herself. *You shouldn't smile with satisfaction at a funeral of a murder victim, especially when you're suspected of the deceased's death and are being observed by the police.* She quickly faced forward, cheeks blazing, and she concentrated on the ceremony before her.

Following a solo and prayer, the congregation was invited forward for a final viewing of the departed, a farewell gesture Claire always avoided. Being able to leave unobserved, rather than almost being late for the service, was the real reason she had sat by herself in the last pew.

Claire paused in the foyer just long enough to slip into her jacket, and as she groped to find a sleeve, someone held the wrap for her, making her awkward struggle easier. Before she could thank the unseen person who had come to her aid, a deep voice said softly in her ear, "So you're still playing detective?"

Claire jerked around to look into the gray eyes of Grant Garrison.

"As were you," she replied indignantly.

"But in my case I'm not playing. Could I buy you a cup of coffee?"

"Do I have any real choice?" Claire asked.

"Of course you have a choice, but I was hoping to talk with you off the record, if you'll permit it."

Claire started to refuse the invitation; her lawyer certainly would have told her to, but curiosity overcame both caution and her dislike of the gray-eyed captain. He was searching for a murderer. What could he want to talk about off the record? Besides, it was in her own best interest to be cooperative.

"All right, I guess," she agreed slowly, "unless you're going to tell me that anything I say can be used against me."

"I won't ask you anything that might incriminate you. I'd like—"

But Garrison was interrupted by the first group to file from the sanctuary. Doctors Evans and Kosvoski were leaving together, and Sydney Andrews was right behind them. The three seemed startled to see Claire and Captain Garrison standing together. Elaine Evans, blotting her eyes, nodded to them; Geraldine Kosvoski looked surprised; and Sydney Andrews frowned.

Rather than waiting for the pallbearers to carry the casket out to the waiting hearse, Garrison steered Claire to his car, leaving Evans, Kosvoski, and Andrews staring after them.

Chapter Nine

Grant Garrison drove to a local coffee shop on West Seventh Street. Even though they were the only customers in the establishment, the captain chose a corner table well removed from the counter and the other tables. As soon as they were seated with steaming mugs in front of them, Claire looked at the captain expectantly, but he hesitated, questioning the wisdom of what he was about to do. Should he really discuss a murder case with the prime suspect? Yet, the prime suspect could well have the clear, uninvolved view of the English department's conflicts that he needed. The department, he had discovered, was highly politicized. Almost everyone had an agenda, an ax to grind. Personal interests and antagonisms were cluttering up the situation and making it difficult to separate the relevant from the irrelevant. However, when he had first spoken with Claire, she told him that although the different factions had approached her, she wasn't receptive and didn't get involved. Her lack of interest in department conflicts had been borne out in interviews with other professors. And he'd noted that even at the funeral, she hadn't joined any of the various cliques but sat alone.

Garrison's long pause made Claire uneasy, and she broke the silence.

"What's our off-the-record conversation going to be about? Are you going to tell me that I'm off the hook because that graduate student Leon Creedmore killed Dr. Rhodes?" she asked hopefully.

"So you've heard about Leon Creedmore, have you? No, he has an airtight alibi."

"His wife, I suppose."

"His wife and every doctor and nurse on duty at the Stillwater Medical Center from early Monday evening until Tuesday morning. His baby was sick—the kid's temperature spiked—and he took him to the emergency room on Monday. He was there at the hospital, loudly complaining and arguing with the nurses, until the child was dismissed the following morning. The coroner puts Rhodes' death during the time Creedmore was at the hospital."

"So if he didn't kill Dr. Rhodes, then I'm still a suspect." The hope drained from her voice as Claire faced the troubling truth.

Captain Garrison took a slow sip of coffee before he

answered. "I'm afraid so. You had means and opportunity. But you are weak in the motive area."

Claire wasn't sure, but Grant Garrison appeared to be teasing.

"Oh, sorry. I'll get right on that and see what I can come up with to incriminate myself!" she offered sardonically. No sooner had she spoken than she was horrified at the way that comment sounded. Once again she silently and forcefully reprimanded herself. *Stop it, Claire! Maybe he's not teasing and doesn't recognize sarcasm when he hears it.*

Garrison, who did recognize the sarcasm, wondered if she would be so quick to joke if she knew someone was trying to provide that motive for her. A second anonymous note stressing the importance of her book to the murder had arrived with the campus mail that morning. He needed to be careful. It would be easy to tell her too much.

Claire was watching him closely and was relieved when he grinned at her.

"I hoped you could help in another way."

"What way's that?"

"I need a better feel for what's going on in your department, and I need it from someone who's not so entrenched in a particular position. I hoped you might be such a person."

"So you'd trust a midnight murderer to become an objective reporter?" she answered in mock disbelief.

Garrison's grin widened. "Yeah. I guess so. At least until you're able to come up with that missing motive."

"Okay. What do you want to know?"

"Apart from the three up for a tenure decision this year—Evans, Kosvoski, and Karns—were there others who feared Rhodes was trying to hurt them in some way?"

"You're asking me to rat out my colleagues."

"I guess I am, but since you like to play detective, I thought you might have made some worthwhile observations."

Claire did like to play detective, and she had made some observations. She salved her conscience by telling herself Garrison probably had already noted the same things and was just trying to confirm what he suspected.

"Well, you've already caught on to the tension between the profs who teach literature and those who are in the technical writing program. I guess there's a real struggle for departmental resources between those groups. Some professors, like Millington, Barnes, and McIntosh, to name a few, think that program should be discontinued. That such a program belongs out at VoTech, not at the university. Rhodes was in that group . . . headed it, I believe."

"But you're not lined up with the literature professors, right?"

"Right. As I told you, I'm trying hard not to be lined up with any departmental faction. I really don't know enough about technical writing to have an opinion one way or the other. But it's hard to believe the division between those two groups was great enough to drive someone to murder."

"Even if one were both on the technical writing staff and up for tenure at the same time?" the captain questioned.

"You mean like George Karns?"

"He comes to mind. Are there any other departmental conflicts besides the fight over technical writing and who gets tenure?"

"None that I've heard about. The only other person I know of who's up for any sort of personnel action is David Stands. He already has tenure, but he's going up for promotion to full professor. And he's not in technical writing."

"But he's after Dr. Millington's graduate classes, isn't he?"

"I don't know. Elaine may have said something to that effect; I'm not sure."

"Were Millington and Rhodes close associates?" Garrison quizzed.

"I don't know how close, but they both were on the graduate faculty. Captain Garrison, you really should be talking to someone who's been at OSU longer than I have."

"But you're the one who told me about the duplicate master key. Dr. Millington didn't volunteer that information when I spoke with him."

"I overheard the secretary say you looked for that key on Friday but couldn't find it."

"Right. But we did track down the secretary Ms. Gooden replaced. A Phyllis Whitman. She's working over in the Development Foundation now. She re-called—" Garrison paused, looking over at the couple who had just entered the coffee shop. Their frayed denim jeans and backpacks suggested they were college students, and their clasped hands suggested they were college students in love. To the captain's relief they sat across the room and were more interested in each other than in any conversation around them. Still, Garrison dropped his voice when he continued. "Ms. Whitman recalled being told about the key when she was hired by Dr. Larkin two years ago. She said the secretary she replaced had it made and kept it in her lap drawer in a metal Band-Aid box. But Ms. Whitman had worked for Dr. Larkin and never had occasion to use it. In fact, she had forgotten about that key until I asked about it."

"So she didn't tell Sue about it when Sue was hired?" Claire questioned, her lowered tone matching Garrison's.

"Apparently not."

"But such a key was made, and now it can't be found?" she asked for confirmation. At Garrison's nod, relief washed over Claire. Millington hadn't been mistaken; his assertion about another master key had been corroborated.

"Right. And it's possible whoever has it was the one who murdered Dr. Rhodes. He—"

"Or she!" Claire interrupted, trying but failing to suppress a grin, so glad she was to learn there had truly been another master key and that Garrison believed it could point to the murderer.

"Or she?" Garrison questioned, frowning at Claire's odd, inappropriate smile. "Aren't you afraid I might discover you had a motive after all?"

"It's hard to find something that doesn't exist. No, I was just remembering something Sydney Andrews said to Geraldine Kosvoski over in the Union the day after Dr. Rhodes' was found. Apparently she takes political correctness seriously, and he was teasing her about it, implying she'd take exception to the automatic assumption the killer had to be a man."

"And did she take exception to that assumption?"

"She took exception to Andrews! I thought for a minute she was going to lean across the table slug him. Luckily David Stands cut in and headed off a confrontation."

Captain Garrison looked thoughtful. "A confrontation, you say. Sounds like Dr. Kosvoski has a short temper. She's up for tenure too, isn't she? And she appears every bit as strong as you, if not more so. Interesting." The gray eyes narrowed.

"That was just an offhand remark," Claire said hastily. "I'm not trying to get Geraldine in trouble. Actually, if she were going to do anyone in, it wouldn't have been Dr. Rhodes. I think she would have been more likely to go after Sydney Andrews."

"Why do you say that?"

"Apparently they dated when she was first hired. Then he dropped her and started seeing the secretary."

"Sue Gooden?"

"Yes, her too, but he also dated the secretary before her. The one you talked to over at the Development Foundation. Phyllis Whitman. Wasn't that her name? According to Geraldine, he hits on every new single female in the department."

"So are you next?" Captain Garrison asked with a half grin.

"I think I may be, and that's probably why Sue has been so abrupt with me lately, but she needn't worry. I'm definitely not interested in Sydney Andrews. But he doesn't seem to have much respect for engagement rings." Claire paused as she noticed Captain Garrison's smile suddenly grow pensive, and she realized she had interrupted him with her remark about political correctness. "I'm sorry. I cut you off. You were saying whoever has that key might be the one who killed Dr. Rhodes?"

Garrison nodded. "If we can correctly assume you are innocent, it would appear that master key was used by the killer, since all the other master keys can be accounted for. After Rhodes was murdered, the killer took his briefcase, which apparently was what he—or maybe she—was after, but didn't want to be seen with.

There were some teaching assistants working late in the building that night. So, using that key, the killer left it hidden in your office, probably with the intention of coming for it later. And it was only the presence of the night crew working on the floors that kept the murderer out of your office."

Claire's cheeks paled. "I hadn't thought of that. If it hadn't been for them, I'd have been there too. I'd gone up to Morrill that night to work but didn't stay because of all the custodians."

"If that crew hadn't been there, I might be investigating two murders instead of one," Garrison said thoughtfully.

It was plain that thought had shaken the young woman, and he quickly changed the subject.

"Okay, so while we finish our coffee tell me about your fellow, this Dirk Drummond, who's in Rome," Garrison invited, wondering, not for the first time, why any man would go off and leave this woman behind.

And for once, Claire didn't find their topic of conversation disagreeable.

Chapter Ten

The day following Dr. Rhodes' funeral and her coffee shop conversation with Captain Garrison, Claire spent the afternoon trying to make her office as presentable as possible, a task she would have completed over the weekend had she not been locked out of the room. She repositioned the desk and computer to better catch the light from the tall south window. The chairs Captain Garrison seemed to find so objectionably masking the fireplace were now set on either side of the grate angled toward one another. A delphinium in a brass pot trailed its green leaves across the mantel, and a bright braided rug lay before the defunct fireplace, lending a bit of warmth to the gray tile floor. Claire was shelving the last box of books when Sydney Andrews rapped on her open door.

"You look busy," he said as he leaned casually against the door frame.

"Oh, hi. Yes. I should have done this weeks ago. But something always kept coming up—like schoolwork." She stopped and pushed her hair back from her sweaty forehead.

"How many new preparations do you have—three, four?" he asked.

"Three, and that's enough to keep me busy. And then I also spent time working on a paper I've submitted for the spring MLA convention."

"Yeah. I remember what first year teaching is like. Before coming here, I taught for a couple of years at a small state college in western Kansas. I had five classes the first semester, and each one was a new preparation. It's tough work until you get a basis of experience under you. And, of course, down here, you're expected to publish."

"It seems to be more of a requirement than an expectation," Claire said, recalling Geraldine Kosvoski's greatest worry apart from not being able to account for herself the night of Dr. Rhodes' murder. Geraldine feared she hadn't published enough to be given tenure.

Sydney glanced at his watch. "It's almost five. I'm surprised you're still here. Most people have cleared out of the building by this time. I guess they're afraid they might be caught alone with Dr. Rhodes' killer."

"Yeah, I've noticed people have been leaving earlier than usual. I'm normally gone by this time too, but I about through here and wanted to get finished. What do you think? Is this an improvement?" she asked, gesturing to her rearranged office.

"Yes. A major improvement. I envy you all of this space. You have room for a small couch in here," he said, surveying the room avariciously. "Rhodes' old office is directly above this, and it's the same size. I wonder who Larkin's going to give it to. I'll have to ask him."

"Isn't it a little soon to think about that? The man is scarcely in his grave," Claire remarked, surprised Sydney was lusting so openly after Rhodes' office this soon after his death.

"You're right. And it's going to take a while before they get it cleaned up. They're probably going to have to replace the tile floor."

"Replace the tile?"

"Blood. It really soaked in the cracks of that old tile flooring. And, of course, it's probably going to need a good airing out," he remarked as he eyed Claire's comfortable office. "I don't have room to swing a cat in my office it's so cramped. Having shelf space for all my books would be great. There's a fireplace in Rhodes' office too, which is a nice touch. Speaking of fireplaces," he said moving toward hers, "is this where they found his briefcase?"

The question didn't surprise Claire. Sydney Andrews wasn't the first person to ask about that. In the week and a half since Dr. Rhodes' death, she had lost track of the number of people who had found a reason to stop by her office door and inquire about the briefcase. And many of these drop-in visitors were from faculties other than English and colleges other than Arts and Sciences. Aggies, engineers, and veterinarians, some from the far west side of the campus, found their way to her door in Morrill Hall.

"Yes, that's the infamous fireplace. I guess the briefcase was stuffed between the artificial logs and the back of the firebox."

"But you're not still under suspicion, are you?" he asked, concerned. "I saw you leave with Captain Garrison after the funeral. I thought for a minute he might be arresting you."

"No. He just had some more questions. Although at one time I think he would have arrested me if he could have come up with a motive. Now I appear to have been demoted from 'a person of interest' to 'a person of waning interest,' even though he told me a copy of my book was in Rhodes' briefcase along with a bunch of other papers."

"Really. Rhodes had a copy of your book? Now that's interesting! You know, that could have been either good or bad, depending on what he was doing with it."

"And if it were bad, I'd likely go back to the top of Garrison's suspect list," Claire said, uncomfortable at the thought.

"And there were other papers in the briefcase too, you say? Did Garrison mention what they were?"

"No, he didn't."

"Evans, Kosvoski, and Karns are wondering if he was looking over their promotion materials. They're up for a tenure decision, and they know he was building a case against them. And, of course, Stands already has tenure, but he's up for promotion to full professor. He was concerned what Rhodes thought of him."

"Why? Was he after Stands too?" Claire asked uneasily, remembering her conversation with Captain Garrison in the coffee shop. Had she accidentally made some passing comment that would make David Stands look bad?

"That's what he's afraid of. Rhodes—not to speak ill of the dead—was an old son of a gun when it came to faculty decisions. Fortunately I made tenure and associate professor last year despite his negative vote. If it hadn't been for my article in *The Oracle*, he'd probably have convinced others to vote against me too."

"Wow! You're in *The Oracle?*" Claire was impressed. *The Oracle* was one of the most prestigious journals in the profession, publishing only the work of the most promising young scholars. *The Oracle* fancied itself the prophesier of those who would most advance the field of literary scholarship, hence its name. "I should be so lucky!" Claire exclaimed. "And you have to make that during your first ten years in the profession, don't you?"

"That's right, but that didn't impress Rhodes. Anyway, by the time I qualify for full professor, he would have been retired, so he was no threat to me. And now

he won't be around to take his scholarly hatchet to you."

Not since someone took his letter opener to him, Claire thought.

"You're probably hungry after all this hard work. How about getting a bite to eat?" Sydney invited with a seductive smile.

"I appreciate the offer, but I'm too hot and tired to be good company. Thanks anyway," Claire said. *Geraldine wasn't wrong*, she thought. *He is trying to hit on me. Waving my engagement ring in his face must be too subtle for him. Okay, I'll be more direct.* "Besides, I'm expecting a call from my fiancé," she added. Actually she wasn't. She and Dirk had already talked at noon when she'd gone home for lunch. But the lie was an easy way to let Sydney know his efforts would continue to be in vain.

"Well, maybe another time. Don't work too late. It's getting dark early and no telling who might be around. I could stay until you're finished," he offered.

"No. That's okay. I'm fine. I'll see you tomorrow," Claire answered, wondering if he didn't know what the word *fiancé* implied. Sydney moved reluctantly out the door, and Claire had the distinct impression he was not accustomed to being turned down.

Frowning, she shoved the last five books into the bookcase. Sydney was acting as if the murderer was prowling the halls. Serial killers aside, some sociologist she had once read contended that most murderers really

weren't a danger to other people. They'd already solved their problems. But what problem could William Rhodes have been to anyone? she asked herself. Perhaps to Elaine Evans or George Karns or Geraldine Kosvoski, since he apparently was spearheading a move to deny them tenure. The job market was very tight right now. If denied tenure, a person was given one more year to find another job before being terminated. *Terminated. That's a final sounding word,* Claire thought with a little shiver. Was it possible one of those three had been so fearful of termination they terminated Rhodes before he could have them terminated? No. That suggested premeditation, and Rhodes' death didn't seem to have been planned. The murder weapon belonged to the victim. Perhaps an argument over tenure had turned ugly, and anger had ripened into violence. But whether it was deliberate murder or unchecked fury, the result was the same: Dr. Rhodes was dead. Whoever said academia was an ivory tower!

Chapter Eleven

Returning to Morrill Hall Friday morning after her class in Ag Hall, Claire walked through waves of sunlight and shadow as the sun played hide-and-seek behind broken clouds. Late fall was not yet ready to give way to winter. The struggle between sun and clouds continued while Claire, back at her desk, used the time before lunch to review for her afternoon class. Her preparation was interrupted by a soft rap on her door, and she looked up at a tall man standing there, a man whose shoulders almost filled the doorway.

"Dr. Markham?" he inquired with a slight hesitant frown.

"Yes?"

"You're a woman!" the tall man exclaimed surprised, but so happily surprised that Claire couldn't take offense.

"The last time I checked," she answered, amused at the man's reaction.

"And a beautiful woman with a sense of humor. I thought a Dr. Markham would be some sour-faced old curmudgeon," the tall man announced with an easy grin as he entered the office and stood before her desk. "And does the delightfully feminine Dr. Markham have a first name?" he asked pleasantly.

"Yes, she does. But she doesn't even know your last name." To her surprise, Claire found herself smiling back at the rugged stranger with closely cropped black hair. The man's easy familiarity was infectious.

"Sorry. I should have introduced myself. I guess I thought the family nose had tipped you off," he said with a quick gesture toward that prominent, but not un-attractive, feature. "I saw you at Dad's funeral. I'm Rob Rhodes," he said, reaching across the desk and offering his hand. His grasp was strong as she expected for someone so solidly built, but she had not expected his large hand to be callused. Retrieving her hand, Claire looked up into his intense blue eyes.

"And you were the late arrival. I saw you too. I'm Claire—Claire Markham. Won't you have a seat?" Claire asked, indicating one of the chairs by the fireplace.

"Thank you. I will." He drew a chair over, settled into it comfortably, and smiled at her. "Claire," he repeated, savoring the word. "That's a beautiful name." As he spoke, his penetrating gaze traveled slowly over her face and frame almost as though he were memorizing what he saw. "Claire. It fits you. A beautiful name for a beautiful woman."

Being referred to as beautiful twice in such a short amount of time by a total stranger left Claire nonplussed, and she struggled for a response, but before she could answer, Rob Rhodes pulled himself from an appreciation of her name and person and back to the conversation. "Yes, you're right. I was late. My brothers had difficulty locating me, but I'm glad I was able to get here for the service."

"Mr. Rhodes, I want you know—"

"Please. It's Rob."

Claire nodded, but she sidestepped his name. She wasn't comfortable calling him by his first name on only a twenty-second acquaintance.

"I'm very sorry about your father. I didn't know him very well—I didn't know him at all, actually—but we all were shocked about the circumstances of his mur—deat—demise," she floundered awkwardly.

"Thank you. Actually, I didn't know him too well, either. I hadn't seen him for a number of years." The tall man smiled at Claire's surprise. "I'm the family black sheep. My brothers didn't expect me to show up either at Dad's funeral or in his will. They were doubly surprised. And to be honest, the latter surprised me too."

Claire was at a loss for a response, feeling that a reference to the prodigal son, while perhaps appropriate, would be less than tactful. She was confused. Why was he telling her things she had no business knowing?

"Is there some particular reason you wanted to see me?" she asked, uneasy with his personal revelations.

"If I'd known how attractive you are, that would have been reason enough." The tall stranger's appraising look once more swept over Claire, this time triggering a faint blush that crept over her cheeks, but he continued without reference to the reaction he had caused. "I'm here because I'm bothered by the lack of progress the police have had in finding Dad's killer. I intend to speak with everyone who had some connection with him. I've just been to see Dr. Larkin, and he mentioned your name—along with a number of others."

Despite the man's rugged charm, Claire quickly decided a preemptive offense was better than a belated defense. She'd let him know she was on to him and that his good-natured familiarity wasn't going to catch her off guard.

"And you sought me out first because Dr. Larkin told you the police have labeled me 'a person of interest,'" she announced flatly, staring into those intense blue eyes.

"Have they?" He sounded surprised. "Dr. Larkin didn't mention that. So you're a 'person of interest.'" Rob Rhodes himself certainly looked interested. His appraising glance sharpened.

Claire sensed his interest centered more on her as a woman than as a murder suspect and that she had told him more than she needed to. But having started down this path, she continued.

"The police are having trouble establishing my guilt. I seem to lack a motive," she explained, attempting a little smile. "In fact, as I've told you, I had no connection whatsoever with Dr. Rhodes."

Rob Rhodes' returned smile was so genuine and his tone so lacking in accusation that Claire could detect no threat in his response.

"Dr. Larkin said you had an appointment with Dad about the time of his death, that his briefcase was found here in your office, and in it was a copy of a book you had written. All that would suggest some sort of connection."

"I suppose it does appear that way. But I have no idea why your father wanted to see me or why he was carrying a copy of my book. I'm sure he would have told me, but he was already gone when I went to his office."

"You found the body?" the tall man asked with a concerned frown.

"No," she hastily answered. "The cleaning crew did that night. Didn't your brothers tell you?"

"My brothers and I don't talk a great deal. They flew home this morning: work to do, children to get back in school. I'm staying to close Dad's house and put it on the market. Apparently we can't leave it unattended."

"Oh?" Claire asked.

"Someone's tried to get in. Tried to force a couple of windows in back, cracked the glass but didn't get inside."

"How awful for your family—that someone would try to break in, especially at this particular time," Claire said sincerely.

"Since my work doesn't require my constant attention, I got tapped for the job of house sitter." The easy smile returned.

Suddenly Claire was very curious about the rugged black-sheep brother with the startlingly blue eyes. What sort of work did he do that didn't require his constant attention but calloused his hands? Whatever it was, it must pay well. His burgundy sweater was cashmere, and he was wearing a Rolex.

"And while I'm here I intend to do some investigating of my own. The campus police don't appear to be coming up with anything," he continued.

Grant Garrison won't be happy to learn he has unwanted outside help, Claire thought. Another critic would only add to the pressure he was under, yet he was the logical person for Rob Rhodes to see.

"I suppose you've talked with Captain Garrison. He's in charge of the investigation." Claire suddenly squinted as the sun broke free of the thick clouds and the sunshine poured through the south window.

"Not yet, but he's on my list—" With a sudden look of awe Rob Rhodes interrupted himself. "You're absolutely stunning," he breathed appreciatively. "When the sun strikes your hair as it is now, it fires a red and gold glow like a halo in a Renaissance painting."

Claire's blush this time was not a faint one. She could feel her cheeks burning at the unexpected and extravagant compliment.

"I hardly qualify for a halo," she murmured, abashed.

"You look like an angel to me," the Rhodes' family black sheep said as he rose and reached for her hand once more. "But forgive me. I've caused you unnecessary concern, embarrassed you, and taken too much of your time. However, if my search warrants it, may I see you again?" he asked, gazing at her hopefully.

Claire found it impossible to deny such a sincere request. "Surely, but I doubt I can be any help to you. And again let me say how sorry I am about your father," she responded with feeling.

"Thank you, Claire Markham," he said, pressing her hand. For the briefest moment Claire thought he was about to lift it to his lips, but instead, with a smile that seemed to promise another meeting, he slowly released it, turned, and left.

Alone in her office, Claire returned to her review of her class notes, but she found it impossible to focus on them: her mind kept drifting to Rob Rhodes. She had never before met a man who so clearly appreciated women and who was so free and natural in his compliments, compliments that appeared genuine. Finally, smiling to herself, she gave up, put her lecture notes aside, and went to the Union for an early lunch.

Chapter Twelve

Having beaten the lunch crowd to the cafeteria, Claire found a table with less difficulty than usual and sat down to eat. The bowl of navy bean soup smelled delicious, and she buttered her first corn muffin. She had taken two with the resolve she'd have just a salad for supper tonight. The older she got the more at home calories threatened to become. She'd hit the weight machines at the Colvin Center this afternoon, she decided. She hadn't gotten over there yesterday, and she'd go back again on Saturday to make up for the missed day. *Might as well,* she thought, *since I still can't leave town.* Surely that prohibition was about to be lifted.

As she slowly sipped her soup, she looked across the crowded room. Near the far wall she saw a familiar face, or at least half of one: she could only see his profile.

Grant Garrison was having an early lunch too, and was talking earnestly with some fellow in a dark suit whose back was to her. As Claire ate, she took a careful look at the man who kept her in town but who no longer appeared to be trying to saddle her with a motive for murder, an impression that allowed her to view the dark-haired captain a bit more objectively. She decided upon closer inspection he wasn't really that bad-looking. Granted, he wasn't as tall or as handsome as Dirk—few men were. Well, Rob Rhodes was taller than Dirk, but not nearly as good-looking as either Dirk or Captain Garrison for that matter, unless one equated ruggedness with good looks.

Claire took a bite of a corn muffin as she considered her morning visitor. She smiled faintly, recalling Rob's overblown, but seemingly sincere, compliments. She also recalled the strength in the callused hand that had twice taken hers. What was it he had said? That he was the family black sheep; that his brothers had difficulty locating him; that everyone was surprised he was included in his father's will.

Her faint smile gradually melted into a faint frown as the seed of an uncomfortable notion occurred to her. Claire probed the troublesome thought. Was it possible? Was that why Captain Garrison was having such difficulty finding Dr. Rhodes' killer? Maybe the killer wasn't connected with the campus in any way. Maybe it was someone whose motive was unknown to anyone except the two parties involved: Dr. Rhodes and, perhaps, his mysterious son. Could that be? The insides of Claire's forearms suddenly prickled with a quick run of goose bumps. Could Rob Rhodes, fearful he was about to be cut from his father's will, have made a surprise visit to the senior Rhodes' office late at night and the homecoming become deadly? Then he suddenly and publicly reappeared for the funeral and now was making a show of being dissatisfied with the efforts of the police, all in an attempt to keep suspicion from himself?

Claire glanced back at Captain Garrison. Should he be made aware of this possibility? In the coffee shop after the funeral, he had asked for her help. That conversation had made her realize the captain wasn't the cold, hard-nosed jerk she had first thought. He was a man with an unpleasant job to do, and he was being pressured to get it done. At least every newspaper from the campus *O'Collegian* through the Stillwater *News-Press* to the *Tulsa World* and the *Daily Oklahoman* from Oklahoma City complained about the lack of progress in the case. The fellow sitting with him could well be someone from the Oklahoma State Bureau of Investigation trying to get him to hand the case over to them. As she looked at him, Claire could almost feel sorry for Grant Garrison. Perhaps she should mention Rob Rhodes to him.

"You seem to be a million miles away. Mind if I sit down?"

Startled from her thoughts, Claire looked up at the

man standing before her table, holding a deli sandwich, a bag of chips, and a Coke.

"Oh. Hi, David. I guess I was. Sure, have a seat."

David Stands set his food on the table and unzipped his blue Windbreaker before sitting down to eat.

"Congratulations. I understand you're no longer the official departmental murderer," the sandy-haired English lit survey professor said with an grin as he opened his chips.

"The official departmental murderer! Is that what people have been calling me?" Claire grimaced.

"Well, you did have Rhodes' briefcase, and the police have been asking about you and won't let you out of town. Can't blame people for trying to put two and two together. But I guess English professors aren't very good at math and came up with the wrong answer. Be that as it may, word did get around."

Apparently it got around more than Claire had realized. She supposed her confinement to Stillwater had been just between her and Garrison or that it had gone no farther than the OSU police.

"But you're saying people no longer think I'm the automatic choice for campus killer, right?" she asked for confirmation.

"Right. Most think if you were, you'd be arrested by now. Especially after you were seen with Garrison at Rhodes' funeral."

"I hadn't realized I was being watched so closely or talked about so much. Maybe people will have someone else to talk about when the police track down that missing master key."

Once more Claire glanced across the room at Grant Garrison. The fact that the briefcase had been found in her locked office was still troubling, and she remembered the captain's comment that whoever had that key might be Rhodes' killer. Suddenly she felt foolish and was grateful she had not gone running to him with her suspicions of Rob Rhodes. Those misgivings were totally unfounded, just as the faculty's had been about her. Rob couldn't possibly have the missing key. He hadn't been around to know about it, let alone be in a position to take it. Someone other than him had hidden the briefcase in her office. Claire was surprised how strangely pleasing that thought was. There was something about the tall, rugged man she found appealing, and she doubted she was the first woman who had felt that way about him. Still, someone had to have that key, and she wondered if Captain Garrison had made any progress tracing it. Finding it would give someone else access to her office and that would put her completely in the clear.

"I don't know anything about a missing master key, but I do know Kosvoski, Evans, and Karns are sweating bullets," Sands commented as he pushed back the lank hair that had fallen over his forehead. "They're sure the police will dream up a motive for one of them. It wouldn't surprise me if all three were guilty."

"All three!" Claire exclaimed, staring at her table

mate in shocked surprise. Then she detected his small, satisfied smile, and Claire realized he was putting her on.

"Sure," he continued. "You know, a sort of *Murder-on-the-Orient-Express* thing because Rhodes was arguing against granting all of them tenure."

"But if I remember the movie correctly, wouldn't all three have had to stab him?" Claire answered, happy to poke a hole in his uncalled-for allusion. It was talk like that that got people in trouble. *So watch your own tongue, Claire,* she told herself, glad once more she hadn't mentioned her suspicion about Rob Rhodes to Captain Garrison.

"Yeah. You're right," Stands agreed. "There was only one stab wound as I recall, so the ménage à trois notion doesn't work in that case."

Claire lifted an eyebrow. "The ménage à trois? In *that* case?" she asked, her tone conveying both her disbelief and disapproval. Careless comments like that were how rumors got started. She had noticed in the past that David Stands often tried to be clever at someone else's expense.

"Okay, wrong term. But according to Sue Gooden, their curriculum vitaes were in that briefcase they found in your office, so it would appear Rhodes was checking into them. Maybe he found something suspect about one of them."

"Surely they can account for where they were the night he was killed. At least Elaine can. She was at home with her husband," Claire said, eager to defend her friend.

"And Karns claims he was at home with his wife and kids. But Kosvoski can't prove where she was, and she's a big woman. She could go bear hunting with a switch."

His flip remark bothered Claire, even though she had made a similar observation earlier, and she answered him more sharply than she intended.

"If muscle is all it takes, then you could have killed Dr. Rhodes."

"But you forget. I already have tenure."

"Yes, but aren't you going up for promotion to full professor? Maybe your promotion materials were in that briefcase too."

"They probably were. Rhodes was a regular Cerberus when it came to personnel issues," he answered easily. "But unlike Geraldine, I have an alibi. I spent that Monday night at home out in the garage working on my car. In fact, my wife hasn't let me hear the end of it. I got battery acid on my suede jacket. Ruined it. Had to throw it out. Joann wasn't happy about that. She had given that jacket to me last Christmas."

"That's too bad," Claire said, remembering the attractive brown jacket he usually wore. She had just taken another spoonful of navy bean soup when another unsettling thought struck her so hard she almost choked. Was she letting her imagination run away with her, or had she just blundered onto another possibility?

Knowing she had just misjudged Rob Rhodes, she realized might she be misjudging David Stands too. Claire quickly reviewed Stands' situation. That unsettling thought could be right, she realized, especially since his jacket was ruined. Suddenly Claire wanted to put as much distance as she could between herself and David Stands. She finished her soup quickly, leaving the second corn muffin uneaten.

"I need to get back. My office hours are about to begin," she said, abruptly excusing herself.

As she hurriedly emptied her tray in the trash receptacle, Claire reviewed that troubling notion. David Stands, whose promotion was being scrutinized by Rhodes, had spent the night of the professor's death out in his garage, out of sight of his wife, for who knew how long. According to David, while he was there, he had ruined his suede jacket with battery acid. But why would anyone wear a good suede jacket while working on a car? Claire didn't doubt the jacket had been ruined, but what had ruined it—battery acid or Dr. Rhodes' blood?

That afternoon until her class began Claire thought about David Stands and his ruined jacket. After class, back in her office, those thoughts returned, and her internal debate resumed. While David's motive might not be as pressing as it was for those who stood to lose their jobs, who knew what might happen if an angry confrontation turned physical in the dead of night in an empty building with no one around to intervene? Should she tell Captain Garrison about the missing jacket or not? Claire asked herself. If she did, would she just be fueling the rumor mill? Stands didn't seem to mind starting stories about others on the faculty, but Claire did. She didn't want to throw suspicion on an innocent man. Yet at the same time, she didn't want the guilty to go free. She hesitated because she almost steered the captain onto Rob Rhodes. Had Garrison still been in the cafeteria when she left, she might have mentioned the missing jacket to him anyway, but the captain and his companion had already left. It was almost five o'clock before she finally decided to call him. But she'd approach the subject gently, she determined, and if he didn't seem receptive, maybe she wouldn't mention it at all. She found Garrison's phone number in the campus directory and dialed. A receptionist answered.

"May I speak with Captain Garrison, please?" she asked.

"Who may I say is calling?" a crisp voice asked politely.

"Dr. Claire Markham from the English department." The receptionist seemed to hesitate, and Claire added quickly, "It concerns the—uh—problem over here."

"One moment, please. I'll buzz him."

Claire heard her call being transferred and a receiver being lifted.

"This is Captain Garrison," a tired voice said.

"Captain Garrison, it's Claire Markham in English. I'm sorry to bother you so late, but I had a question."

"Yes?" The voice didn't sound quite so tired.

"I wondered, would it be possible for whoever stabbed Dr. Rhodes not to have gotten bloody?"

"Possible perhaps, but not very likely. Why?"

"So if a person who had a really nice jacket suddenly stopped wearing it, would that make you suspicious?"

"I think it's making *you* suspicious. But maybe that jacket is just at the cleaners."

"No, it's not at the cleaners. It's been thrown out. He said he got battery acid on it."

"Is this person on the faculty over there?" His voice sharpened with interest.

"Yes."

"Did this person have a reason to be angry at Dr. Rhodes?"

"Possibly."

"Does this person have an alibi?"

"Yes, but it's weak."

"Are you in your office?"

"Yes."

"Stay there. I'll be right over!"

And the phone went dead in Claire's ear.

Chapter Thirteen

Claire was surprised how rapidly Grant Garrison made it from his office in the USDA building on the west side of the campus to hers on the second floor of Morrill Hall on the far east side.

"You're about the only one left in the building," he said as they moved to the chairs before the fireplace. "Except for the secretaries in the main office, the place seems empty."

"You're right. People have been leaving early ever since Dr. Rhodes' death. And then this is Friday afternoon; people always leave early on Fridays. Me too, usually. I guess was distracted trying to decide whether or not to call you. I'm probably just imagining things." Earlier that day Claire had seen guilt where there wasn't any, and she hoped she wasn't doing so once more.

"Maybe, maybe not," he responded. "Okay, now tell me about this jacket. Whose was it? How did you find out it had been ruined?"

Hesitantly, still not sure she was doing the right thing by casting doubt on David Stands, Claire repeated her lunch conversation with the English lit professor.

Garrison listened closely. "So he said he threw it out; he didn't say he burned it?"

"Right."

"And he was at home working on his car the night of Rhodes' death."

"That's what he said."

"Could his wife verify he was in the garage all that time—that he didn't take the car out for a test drive?"

"She might be able to. I didn't ask."

"He wouldn't happen to have an unattached garage by any chance, would he? Maybe one out at the back of the lot away from the house?"

"I wouldn't know. I only know he lives somewhere in the old College Circle addition."

"Are you the only one he's mentioned his jacket to?"

"I wouldn't know that, either. But he used to wear it all the time. It was a really nice brown suede jacket. I suppose someone might have noticed he wasn't wearing it. Why?"

"I'm concerned that if I mentioned the missing jacket to him he could trace the source of my interest back to you."

"I hadn't thought about that," Claire murmured uneasily.

"If he should be the killer, it wouldn't be good if he knew who fingered him. If he's not, then he might bear resentment against you for telling me about him. It might make it difficult for you to work with him in the future."

"That's something else I hadn't thought about," Claire answered, a worried frown drawing a furrow between her dark green eyes. "But David Stands doesn't have much more of a motive than I have," she said, suddenly embarrassed she had mentioned him and his jacket to Captain Garrison. "He wasn't in danger of losing his job. It was just a promotion. Besides, I can't imagine him finding Dr. Rhodes in his office late at night and attacking him."

"It was the other way around."

"What do you mean?"

"Whoever killed Rhodes was already in his office looking for something, and Rhodes surprised him—or her," he added, his voice tinged with a faint suggestion of amusement.

"*Him* is fine. I won't insist on equal billing when it comes to murder. I'll leave that to Geraldine Kosvoski."

"Who, if I recall what Stands said, 'could go bear hunting with a switch.' He doesn't seem hesitant to throw suspicion on another faculty member."

"Nor do I, obviously," Claire answered uncomfortably. "I guess everyone is looking at everyone else askance, including me. But why do you think Rhodes walked in on the killer instead of the killer going to his office to confront him?"

Garrison hesitated a moment before responding. "We haven't made this public knowledge yet, so I'd appreciate you keeping it quiet. Rhodes' desk had been ransacked; drawers in the file cabinet were left open, and we found a flashlight that had rolled under the desk. It had been left on; the batteries were dead."

"So there should have been plenty of fingerprints!" Claire said eagerly.

"There were plenty of fingerprints. Rhodes had a number of people in his office recently, which makes moot the results of fiber and hair tests."

Claire recalled the series of interviews Rhodes had been conducting. A number of people had recently been in his office. She herself had an appointment, which had been unkept; therefore, none of the fibers and hair that were analyzed could have belonged to her. That certainly should put her in the clear. Before she could call this to his attention, Garrison continued.

"But no fingerprints were found where they shouldn't have been. And none were on the flashlight or the letter opener. Looks like the killer wore gloves, as most people seem to these days if they plan on doing something they shouldn't."

"What about the flashlight? Could it be traced?"

"It's the kind sold at Wal-Mart. Nothing distinctive about it."

"Since the killer was already in Rhodes' office, that proves someone had a master key, doesn't it?" Claire asked excitedly. "And that means I'm not the only one who could get into this office. I'm completely off the hook!" she exclaimed with relief. "Why didn't you tell me?"

"I wasn't sure until last night."

"What happened last night?"

"You remember I said I was reading your book."

"Yes."

"Last night, I got to the analysis chapter where you compared Comfort's handwritten manuscripts to the earlier published stories and demonstrated he couldn't have written them. Rhodes had made some marginal notes, so small and faint I missed them when I first thumbed through the book."

"What sort of marginal notes?"

"Comments like 'Neatly done' and 'Excellent observation.' It looks like you had nothing to fear from him. He may have scheduled your appointment to compliment you on your work. If so, he probably would have supported you for tenure and promotion when that time came. He'd be the last person you'd want to see dead."

Claire was doubly surprised and pleased: both that she was no longer a suspect and that Dr. Rhodes had found her work commendable.

"He had written that?" she asked, smiling with pleasure. "I had no idea; he always came across so superior and distant that I never would have guessed. Others in the department were worried what he thought about them."

"Yes. And it looks as though one of them wanted something they thought might be in his briefcase, since that's all that was taken."

Claire's green eyes narrowed as she imagined the scene. "Dr. Rhodes was both surprised and angry to find the person in his office going through his things, and I suppose they started arguing."

"Safe assumption. Then the argument got physical, and during the struggle, the intruder got his hands on the letter opener and used it."

"Which would suggest it wasn't a premeditated killing. The intruder hadn't come with a weapon."

"It may not have been premeditated, but it was murder. And the fact that Rhodes died as a result of the burglary makes it murder one. Then the killer grabbed the briefcase and left."

"And he must have left in a hurry because he didn't take the flashlight," Claire said, continuing the story.

"So, using that master key once again, he hid the briefcase in here behind those logs," Garrison said, glancing at the firebox, "with the intention of getting it later. As disordered as this place was then, he probably thought it wouldn't be seen here."

"But he couldn't get it because during the day, I was

here, and that night the custodial crew was waxing floors—until they found Dr. Rhodes' body."

"And then the place was full of police."

"And that's why the contents of Rhodes' briefcase are so important," Claire mused. "Something in it was worth someone's life." Claire caught Captain Garrison looking at her strangely, and she hastened to add, "Something other than my book, of course."

"Of course. If I thought you were involved, I wouldn't be sitting here reconstructing the crime with you."

"Does this mean I'm no longer 'a person of any sort of interest'? Am I free to leave town?" she asked sharply.

"Yes, it does. I intended to call you this morning and tell you, but I got busy early and was just winding up when you called. Apart from Thanksgiving, I hope you weren't inconvenienced too much."

"Thanksgiving was quite enough, thank you," she answered coolly. "I was afraid you weren't going to let me out of town for Christmas either."

"No, you're free to come and go as you please," Grant Garrison said impassively, although he wished he could keep her in town if it meant he could have Christmas dinner with her too.

"You have no idea how good it is to have my life back and no longer be a suspect," Claire said, drawing a long breath. "Still, someone was the murderer, someone on campus, maybe someone in the department. The grapevine says Dr. Rhodes was carrying tenure and promotional materials for the four people up for personnel action."

"The grapevine is right, for a change." Garrison paused as though uncertain to continue before he asked, "Does the name Haskell Billingham mean anything to you?"

"Haskell Billingham? No, there's no one by that name on the English faculty."

"Or on the whole OSU faculty, for that matter. Have you ever heard of a student by that name?"

"No. But as I've said before, I'm a poor one to ask. I haven't been here that long."

"And Dr. Wells, the departmental advisor, couldn't find a record of any former English student by that name either."

"Why do you ask?"

"The only thing in Rhodes' briefcase that didn't relate to someone on the English faculty was a paper written by a Haskell Billingham."

"What was the paper about?"

"William Faulkner. It's entitled 'Flem Snopes: American Everyman.' "

"Really! That's an unpleasant thought! I mean Flem Snopes as Everyman, not Haskell Billingham," Claire hastened to clarify. "Dr. Rhodes was just beginning a two-year stint as the editor of an English journal called *The Oracle*. Perhaps this Mr. Billingham had submitted the paper for publication, and Dr. Rhodes just happened to have it with him."

"You may be right," Garrison agreed. He rose and smiled tiredly at her. "It's getting late, and I've kept you long enough. I appreciate your telling me about Stands' jacket. We'll follow up on that."

"You're welcome, I guess," Claire muttered, still wondering if she had done the right thing. "I'd better be going too," she said, rising and reaching for her leather jacket that hung on the coat tree by the door.

"Here. Let me help you with that," he said, once more taking the dark jacket and holding it for her.

As she button it up and drew her long green scarf under her collar, Claire caught Garrison looking closely at the front of her jacket.

"Checking for blood?" Claire asked archly. "I thought you said I was no longer a suspect."

To her surprise, the man blushed.

"Sorry. It's . . . it's a habit that comes with the job, I'm afraid," he muttered, embarrassed yet grateful she had mistaken the reason for his scrutiny. It was not his habit to ogle women, and to his shame, he just had.

Chapter Fourteen

True to her resolve at lunch, Claire ate only a salad
that evening, although since she'd left the second corn
muffin uneaten, she topped the lettuce and fresh
spinach with a little grated cheese and some shaved
ham. She ate slowly, thinking about her conversation
with Grant Garrison. Her calico cat KayCee, annoyed
she was taking so long with her supper, jumped onto
her lap and repeatedly nosed under her hand, demanding to be petted. At length Claire pushed her salad away
and absently began stroking KayCee under her chin and
scratching behind her ears. The cat, unconcerned about
murders and murderers, purred contentedly, kneading
her front paws.

"You don't have a thing to worry about, do you,
KayCee? So long as you have food in your dish, water

in your bowl, and someone to pet you when you want it, you're satisfied," Claire said, stroking the large cat that filled her lap. "You don't have to worry about falsely accusing someone of murder."

Troubled by that thought, Claire began second-guessing herself. If David Stands wasn't the killer, who was? Rhodes surely didn't stick that letter opener in his own carotid artery. With no master key, his son couldn't have gotten into his father's office, nor left the briefcase in hers. Barring some angry student, until her conversation with David Stands that day, the only obvious contenders for the title were those who feared they might lose their jobs: Geraldine Kosvoski, Elaine Evans, and George Karns. All three had been on campus long enough that one of them might have blundered onto the missing master key.

It didn't seem possible that even-tempered, petite Elaine could have killed Dr. Rhodes. If she had gotten into a physical fight with him, she would have lost. Besides, her husband said they had been home all night. George Karns' wife had said the same thing. Of course, spouses might lie even under oath. But Geraldine Kosvoski had no one who could attest to her whereabouts that night, and she might well have been able to best Dr. Rhodes in a struggle. Assuming that Jack Evans, husband of her friend Elaine, and Anne Karns, wife of technical writing professor George, were telling the truth, that left only Geraldine Kosvoski, Claire reasoned. At least she had been the only remaining suspect until Claire had talked with David Stands that day. Might he have had a violent confrontation with Dr. Rhodes concerning his promotion prospects? Once more, Claire's troubled mind circled back to the English lit professor, his missing jacket, and what she had observed as she drove home from the campus this evening.

After working out at the Colvin Center before leaving the campus, she had detoured through the old College Circle neighborhood where David and his wife lived. The homes there were all one-story bungalows, probably built in the early twenties. All had detached garages, many accessed through alleys. It could have been possible for Stands to have left for a short time and his wife not know it. She had been right in telling Garrison about David's missing jacket, Claire told herself. He could well be the killer. Unless it was a distraught student or someone who had a reason no one knew about. But if that were the case, how did someone not connected with the department get a master key? And why did the killer take the briefcase and hide it?

Claire's thoughts shifted to what the briefcase contained. The stray paper found there bothered her. While the name Haskell Billingham meant nothing to her, the title of his paper, "Flem Snopes: American Everyman" nagged at her. Had she heard it before? The more she thought about that title, the more familiar it sounded. Well, not the exact title so much as the idea the title expressed, she decided. It was probably something she had read in grad school and had no bearing on the investigation going on at Oklahoma State.

KayCee, deciding she had enough adoration for the moment, swatted Claire's hand away lightly and leaped from her lap. The cat strolled regally into the front room where she sat down to attend to matters of feline hygiene. Claire rinsed her salad bowl at the kitchen sink and added it to the collection in the dishwasher. As she was reaching for the detergent, the phone rang. The call was from Dirk. Because of the time difference with Rome, they didn't talk long, but long enough for Claire to share the good news that the police no longer considered her a murder suspect and for her to be assured she was missed and loved. She went to bed smiling.

Saturday morning, as Claire poured herself a bowl of cereal, she glanced first at the kitchen calendar and then out the window. The day promised to be a crisp one of vivid blue skies and bright sunlight. Nothing in the weather suggested Christmas was fast approaching, a fact Dirk had called to her attention last night during their brief conversation. His comment made her realize how preoccupied she had been with the Rhodes murder and her own erstwhile suspected involvement in it. She had been oblivious to the garlands of greenery that festooned the halls of the Student Union and the carols on the radio. Now that her confinement to the city limits of Stilllwater was revoked, the day looked like a perfect time for a Christmas shopping trip to Oklahoma City.

Elaine happily accepted Claire's invitation to join her, and the two spent the day hitting three of the city's main malls: Quail Springs, Penn Square, and Crossroads. They returned home late Saturday evening happy and tired, pleased with their purchases. Elaine had spent most of her money in Toys "R" Us, buying gifts for her nieces and nephews. Claire, who had no young relatives, walked the laden shelves wondering if someday she and Dirk would have a little boy or girl to shop for.

It was in other stores where Claire made her purchases. For her mother, she selected a black leather purse and for her father, the Lewis and Clark volumes he'd been admiring. Finding a present for Dirk had been more difficult. He had dropped no hints about what he'd like, and when Claire had asked him directly, he had laughed and replied, "Whatever you want me to have. If it's from you, I'll love it." So what did she want him to have? Something that would last and showed how much she loved him, she decided. She settled on a rich masculine bracelet of heavy gold links. The expensive gift nearly maxed out her charge card, but she didn't care. The more she looked at the gleaming chain, the more she knew it was the perfect gift.

Sunday Claire spent the day writing Christmas cards and updating her friends and family on her year's activities, though she didn't mention the current difficulty on campus or her involvement in it. Murder didn't seem an appropriate message for a Christmas note, she decided. As she wrote, her eyes kept drifting to her desk calendar and the heavily circled December date: the date Dirk would return. Each time she looked at it, she grinned. Monday morning when Claire stopped by the main English office to leave her stamped Christmas cards in the "Mail Out" tray, she found a small cluster of faculty gathered around Dr. Larkin, discussing the police investigation of students Rhodes had recently failed.

"Yeah, I heard Leon Creedmore had an alibi," Dr. Wells, the short, bespectacled departmental advisor, was saying.

"Yes, his whereabouts during the time of Dr. Rhodes' death can be accounted for," Dr. Larkin agreed.

"Well, I know he failed more than just one student," Geraldine Kosvoski interjected, brushing her mousey brown hair back from her broad face.

"And they've been checking them," Dr. Wells answered. "Two now live out of state—in Oregon and South Dakota. Another fellow is in Iraq with his National Guard unit."

Claire noticed Geraldine frown at that news. *She must know she's a suspect and is hoping for some more company*, Claire thought. *I know just how she feels.* Although Claire had had no motive, neither did she have anyone who could confirm her whereabouts the night of the murder, and that had been coupled with the inescapable fact that Rhodes' briefcase was found in her locked office. Silently she gave a little prayer of thanks that Garrison finally recognized her innocence.

"Two others are still on campus, but their fraternity brothers say they were at the house all that night," Dr. Burrows added. Lee Burrows, the linguistics professor, also served as faculty advisor to that particular fraternity house. Claire thought Burrows was a good fit for that job. He obviously enjoyed it, and he looked like a fortyish fraternity boy himself. To Claire he was the departmental peacock, inordinately proud of his heavy wavy hair and aquiline profile.

"Are they still passing around those research paper files over there?" Sydney Andrews asked. "That's what got those two guys in trouble with Rhodes."

Dr. Burrows, taking exception to Andrews' implied criticism of his role at the fraternity house, started to reply, but Douglas McIntosh, who for thirty years had specialized in Romantic poetry, cut him off.

"What about that big, burly fellow last year who was going to be an English major until Rhodes flunked him? I can't recall his name, but he was a big strong guy."

"You probably mean Arnold Meltzer," Dr. Wells answered. "The police interviewed him, and he doesn't have an alibi for that night."

"So are they going to arrest him?" Sydney asked.

"I don't think so. His right arm is in a cast from the shoulder to the wrist. Motorcycle accident. And he's on crutches," Wells added.

"William's been dead for two weeks, and the OSU police haven't made any progress on this case," McIntosh interjected, his dark eyes snapping with pent-up frustration. "If they don't come up with something soon, they should be forced to hand the investigation over to an agency that can get something done, like the OSBI," he announced angrily, and everyone in the group murmured their agreement.

"I mean, the OSU police handle parking violations, crowd control, and the occasional drug overdose fine, but something like murder seems to be beyond them," McIntosh continued. "And I'm not the only one who thinks so. One of William's sons—that big tall one; I think his name is Robert—has been over complaining to Garrison."

Claire didn't listen any further. She picked up her mail, two circulars from textbook companies, suffered a scowl from Sue, and left for her own office. For the first time she felt truly sorry for Grant Garrison. But maybe finding Stands' discarded jacket would be the break he needed. Over the weekend the news media had announced that the OSU police was beginning to search the local landfill.

The police landfill search was the topic of discussion that noon as Claire and Elaine Evans had lunch in the cafeteria. Claire was very careful what she said, pretending no more knowledge about the search of the city dump than anyone else in the department. She had taken Garrison's concern for her anonymity to heart.

"I wonder what they're looking for," Elaine said, blotting her mouth with a paper napkin.

Claire's answer was a noncommittal shrug.

"And I wonder *why* they started looking. Something or someone must have given them a tip of some sort," her friend added.

"I suppose so," Claire replied. "A search like that has got to be a dirty job, a real mess."

"Speaking of real messes, I narrowly avoided one," Elaine volunteered.

"What do you mean?" Claire asked, surprised.

"Thank heaven I have someone other than just Jack to attest to where I was the night Dr. Rhodes was killed. Husbands, apparently, don't count for much when it comes to alibis."

"Don't tell me the police actually thought you might have killed Dr. Rhodes! The man must have outweighed you by more than a hundred pounds. There's no way you have overpowered him!" Claire exclaimed.

"But there's no telling what the police might think when they're getting desperate. Fortunately there's a positive side to having a backed-up sewer. I also have a plumber who can say where I was that night and an overtime bill to prove he was there," Elaine said with satisfaction.

And Claire, who had no husband, plumber, or bill to prove her whereabouts, once more was grateful Captain Garrison knew she was innocent. However, if he were forced to hand the case over to the OSBI, would that agency share his conviction? Claire wondered uneasily. Almost as though thinking about the OSU police captain had conjured him up, Grant Garrison suddenly appeared at her elbow and spoke to her quietly before moving on.

Elaine looked at her, puzzled. "What was that all about?" she asked.

"Very little, I'm afraid," Claire answered and quickly changed the subject to the problem of who was going to take over Dr. Rhodes' courses. But to Garrison it hadn't been very little, Claire knew, as she recalled his words: "Found it. It's battery acid."

Chapter Fifteen

"**B**attery acid. Not blood," Claire repeated to herself that evening as she sat staring dully at the TV screen, too preoccupied to notice the rerun of crab fishermen risking death on the Discovery Channel or the large cat in her lap. KayCee, annoyed she was being ignored, moved to the couch beside Claire and began pulling maintenance on her claws, gnawing at them and licking between her extended toes. Satisfied with the job she had done, the cat folded her front paws under her chest and blinked slowly, about to go to sleep.

Claire was not so satisfied with herself. She was feeling guilty. The front page of the *Stillwater NewsPress* ran a large headline: LANDFILL SEARCH HALTED. She was the one whose observations had sent Grant Garrison and his force on that wild goose chase. Garrison, already exhausted and harassed, had wasted time and manpower on a most unpleasant, fruitless task, and she was to blame. If she hadn't been so ashamed of herself, she would have called him to apologize.

But since Stands' alibi held up, then who killed Dr. Rhodes? Geraldine Kosvoski was the last likely person with no supportable alibi for her presence the night of the murder. Yet, even given that fact and her apparent strength, Claire had a hard time imagining her as the killer. What reason would she have for searching Dr. Rhodes' office? The only thing in the briefcase pertaining to her was her curriculum vitae, and there was nothing secret about that. That document was available to all the faculty to help them decide if she was tenure worthy. Obviously there was something in that briefcase the killer had wanted; the briefcase was all he took. If so, whatever it was would point to the killer. But what could it have been? Claire's query was interrupted by the insistent ringing of her phone.

"Markham residence," she said, picking up the receiver and hoping the caller was Dirk.

"Then this must be Claire Markham," a deep, warm voice rumbled in her ear.

The resonant, masculine voice was not Dirk's, and Claire struggled to place it.

"It's Rob Rhodes. We met Friday. I'm here at Dad's, and I said I'd call if I needed help."

"But, as I recall, I said I really doubted I could help you."

"I hope you can with this. How do you scramble eggs?"

"Scramble eggs!" Claire exclaimed, totally taken aback.

"How do you keep the egg shells out of the eggs when you crack them? And how much oil do you put in the skillet when you cook bacon?"

"You don't put any oil in the skillet when you're frying bacon; bacon produces its own grease as it cooks. When it's done you drain the grease on a paper towel, and then scramble the eggs in the same skillet. There will be enough grease left to keep them from sticking, and it will flavor the eggs," she directed.

"Okay. That makes sense. Now how do I get the eggshells out of—Oh. Is raw bacon supposed to be green?"

"No! That means it's spoiled. Don't try to eat it! Throw it out."

"Tell you what. Why don't I just throw it all out, and let's go out to eat? I'm sick of eating cold cereal and baloney sandwiches. Is there any place in town where we can get a decent omelet at night?"

"You can get a good omelet at IHOP. It's on the east side of Main Street between McElroy and Hall of Fame. It's not hard to find."

"Okay. I'll meet you there in thirty minutes."

"Thanks anyway, but I'm good," Claire said even though her stomach growled in disagreement.

"Have you already eaten?"

"No."

"Look. I can't cook, and even if I could, I don't like to eat alone. But beyond that, I want to show you something. While I've been going through Dad's things, I've found some letters—notes, actually—that I'd like to ask you about."

"If it's anything that might relate to your father's death, you should take them to Captain Garrison," Claire advised.

"Captain Garrison doesn't seem to think too much of me. I guess I rubbed him the wrong way when we talked last week. I can't tell if these might pertain to Dad's death or not. I don't know how things operate at a university. Maybe you could tell if they're important or if I should just throw them away."

"Notes, you say?" Claire's curiosity was pricked, and she was sorely tempted to have supper with the Rhodes family black sheep despite his blatant flattery Friday morning in her office.

"Yes, seven of them, all from the same person."

"Really. What's the name?"

"I'll tell you that when we've finished our omelets. See you at IHOP in thirty minutes," Rob Rhodes said confidently before hanging up the phone.

So supper with Rob Rhodes was the price she would have to pay to see notes that might relate to Dr. Rhodes' death. If they did, that would do two things: put her well beyond any suspicion, even if the OSBI did end up with the case, and it would help Grant Garrison, especially since her tip about the jacket hadn't worked out.

Claire went into the bathroom to freshen up, and as she was brushing her teeth, she grimaced at a contradictory fact: she had turned down Sydney's dinner invitation, yet she was willing to meet Rob Rhodes for a meal. Then the grimace faded as quickly as it had come. The two situations were completely different. Sydney had asked her for a date; Rob was asking for help in solving a crime, help she had earlier agreed to. Besides, she hadn't had supper, and she was hungry.

Wiping her mouth, she glanced in the mirror and stopped in dismay. The front of her navy blue sweatshirt was covered in cat hair that resisted her attempts to brush it off. It was Claire's turn to be annoyed.

"Thanks a bunch, KayCee! No one's going to want to eat while sitting across the table from a shirt full of cat fur. Now I've got to change."

Since her only other sweatshirt without holes was in the laundry hamper, Claire traded her jeans and cat-hair-covered sweatshirt for tan slacks and a green turtleneck. She quickly brushed her heavy, shoulder-length hair and refreshed her lipstick before hurrying to her car.

Driving to the restaurant, she began questioning her willingness to see Rob Rhodes. It was one thing to want to help him, but why was she so eager to get there? Was it because she wanted to see the notes he had discovered, or was it because she found the rugged, self-confessed black sheep more interesting than she wanted to admit? Was she more susceptible to his flattery than she realized? If so, she and Dirk really had been apart too long. Claire was frowning as she swung into the IHOP parking lot; then her face cleared. It was only the notes. They were what brought her here, the notes and a raging curiosity.

Rob was waiting for her when she arrived at the pancake house. She slid into the booth across from him before he could rise.

"Are you really going to make me wait until we've eaten before you show me what you've found?" she asked.

"And hello to you too," he answered, grinning. "You look especially nice this evening. That green sweater matches your eyes."

"Yeah, yeah, yeah. And when the sun hits my hair I have a halo," she responded dismissively with a grin of her own. "Now, what about the notes?"

"What about ordering and eating first? What looks good?" he asked, picking up a menu.

There was no dissuading him. Food came first: the largest omelet on the menu for him with extra sides of jalapeño peppers and ham and the smallest omelet for her with dry whole-wheat toast. Rob obviously enjoyed the big omelet, which he ate with gusto. Claire had the impression he did everything with gusto. The man radiated energy. She imagined him at the Rhodes house, ripping through closets and cupboards, blithely clearing out the accumulation of his father's lifetime. Without warning or conscious volition, her mind flashed on another image: Rob joyfully covering a nude blonde who writhed happily under him, her tumbled curls cascading over the pillow and his forearms. The unexpected image caused Claire's cheeks to suddenly flush, and Rob noticed as she hurriedly reached for her water glass.

"You okay?" he asked.

"Yes. No problem. I think a piece of your jalapeños must have gotten in my omelet," she lied between sips of water, silently thankful the imagined woman, who was so enthusiastically enjoying Rob's attention, had blond rather than reddish brown hair.

"Really? They're not all that hot. You should try them down in Mexico," he answered with a grin.

"Do you go to Mexico often?" Claire asked in an attempt to direct the conversation toward him. But despite her best efforts she learned next to nothing about him, while he learned a good deal about her and the man who had given her the engagement ring with the large diamond.

"So he's in Rome, making a film. I'm impressed. I've been told that's harder work than it would appear. Who's the director?" Rob asked.

"Richard Steele."

"Honestly? I know Richard. In fact, I saw him shortly before I got the word about Dad."

"You were in Rome?"

"Right."

"On business?" Claire was determined to learn something definite about him.

"Business, pleasure, a bit of both, I suppose. I visited Richard on the set, met several people there."

"Was one of them named Dirk Drummond?"

"Dirk Drummond? Yes, I believe so. Blond hair with a faint red cast, yellowish brown lion's eyes, well-built?"

"Yes, that's Dirk," Claire answered thoughtfully, wondering if perhaps her picture of Rob and a blonde woman was incorrect. He certainly had checked Dirk out. Was that because he was more interested in men than women?

"I know what you're thinking, and don't read anything into that," Rob said with a wolfish grin.

Claire was startled he could read her thoughts so easily, and she felt a flush of embarrassment as she fumbled a denial. "No. Not really. I—"

"That's okay. It's an understandable error, but I've found it necessary to observe people closely and notice unusual features. For example, the remarkable reddish glow of your hair, your clear emerald eyes, that little black mole at the left corner of your lower lip, not to mention your—"

This time it was Claire's turn to interrupt; his eyes had traveled from that mole to her green sweater. Claire was eager to turn the conversation from either him or herself and quickly returned to Dirk.

"So you've met Dirk. Was he . . . well?" That wasn't the question Claire wanted to ask. She wanted to know if Dirk was behaving himself, but to ask that would suggest she didn't trust him, and if she didn't trust him, their relationship was in jeopardy.

"Very well, he's a director's dream, Richard told me. Always on time; always prepared; always open to direction." Rob grinned. "You know, this is a small world, isn't it? Little did I know when I met him that a short time later I'd be eating omelets with his fiancée in Stillwater, Oklahoma, of all places."

The flood of questions that crowded Claire's mind remained unasked. Of course she could trust Dirk, she told herself, just as he could trust her.

When the plates were cleared and fresh cups of coffee poured, Rob reached inside his sport jacket and removed seven white envelopes. But Claire didn't notice what he set on the table. She was focused on the glint of metal under his left arm that she glimpsed when he opened his jacket for the envelopes.

"These aren't—" Rob paused, noting the wide-eyed shock on Claire's face. "What's wrong?" he asked. "Can't be another jalapeño. The waitress took our plates."

"Is that what I think it is?" Claire whispered, eyeing what she perceived to be a slight bulge in his jacket.

"That depends on what you think it is," he replied.

"You're carrying a gun!" she whispered.

"Right. And don't look so worried. I have a permit."

"I'm not worried. I'm just surprised. Apart from the

police, I've never seen anyone carry a handgun before," she explained. *Nor have I ever known anyone who needed to,* she thought. *Well, maybe Dr. Rhodes should have*, she amended to herself.

"Old habits can be useful. Saturday night while I was out, someone tried to break in again."

"Again? To your father's house?"

"Yeah. This time whoever it was tried to jimmy the glass door on the patio. Dented the metal door frame pretty badly. So far no one's gotten in, but should they manage to, I don't intend to be caught as unprepared as Dad was."

"Have you called the police?" Claire asked.

By way of an answer, Rob threw her a disgusted look, which reenforced her impression of his low opinion of the police, city as well as campus.

"Do you think the prowler could be the same person who attacked your father? Someone who's still after something your father had?"

"I think that's a reasonably safe assumption. And since the police aren't making any headway, I want to find that person as soon as possible. That's why I wanted you to look at these notes," Rob said, gesturing to the small stack of envelopes on the table. "These aren't dated, so I'm guessing at the order Dad received them from what they say." He opened the first envelope, removed the crisp folded note paper, and handed it to Claire.

The brief note, written in heavy black ink, expressed

the writer's concern for the early fall cold Dr. Rhodes was suffering from. It was signed with only the initials G. K. written in a distinctive backward slant.

"Who is G. K.?" Claire asked, looking up into the vivid blue eyes that were watching her closely.

"I was hoping you could tell me."

"Is that how all the notes are signed?"

"Yes. And there's no address on any of the envelopes."

"So your father must not have gotten them through the regular mail. My guess is that G. K. must have put them in his mailbox at the English office."

"Which would suggest that G. K. is someone in the English department. Any idea who that might be?"

Claire frowned thoughtfully. "It could be Geraldine Kosvoski, I suppose. But why are you curious? The writer's only concerned about your father's health."

Instead of answering, Rob handed her the next note, which expressed the writer's continuing concern over Dr. Rhodes' persistent cold and offered to bring over a pot of chicken soup.

"I don't see anything sinister here," Claire said as Rob gave her a third note. His easy manner was gradually turning grim.

Claire frowned as she read the innuendo in the third message. If the chicken soup hadn't warmed him enough, the writer was willing to personally do the warming.

"Well, it's a woman, so we know it's probably Geraldine," she said, laying that note aside.

"Do we?"

"I just naturally thought . . ." Claire's voice trailed away in embarrassment as Rob offered the fourth envelope.

Reading between the lines, Claire inferred that G. K. had been taken up on that personal offer. The carefully worded note suggested the two had spent a night doing something other than eating chicken soup and that G. K. was impressed with the elder Rhodes' stamina.

Rob gave her a fifth note, which Claire didn't open.

"I shouldn't be reading these. I have no business knowing this sort of thing about your father," Claire said firmly.

Rob opened the note for her and pointed to the distinctive initial signature.

"Does the handwriting look familiar?"

"No," she answered looking at the backward-sloping initials. Despite her protest that she didn't want to read Dr. Rhodes' private correspondence, Claire quickly scanned the fifth brief message. It was another note of appreciation for "a night in paradise." Clearly more than chicken soup was involved.

"Is Kosvoski the only person in your department with those initials?" His voice was rough with scarcely controlled emotion.

"No," Claire answered hesitantly. "There's George Karns. Of course, the writer wouldn't have to be on the faculty. It might have been a student. Someone willing to do whatever for a good grade."

"I don't think it was a student," Rob said as he

handed her a sixth note. "This sounds like whoever it was wanted something other than a grade. He or she wanted some sort of endorsement."

Claire read the note that indicated what the writer wanted in return for being such a cooperative and silent partner. Rob's was right; something other than a grade was wanted. The note read, *"Dear one. During the upcoming process, I trust you'll be as strong in your support for me as you were in bed last night. G. K."*

"Do you have any idea what this G. K. is referring to besides an affair with my father?" Rob asked.

"I think so. Geraldine Kosvoski is up for a tenure decision this year. If she doesn't get it, she'll have only one more year to teach before being let go. I've heard rumors she's afraid her publication record isn't strong enough to have her contract renewed. Your father was the head of the reappointment committee and was very influential with a lot of the faculty, so—"

"And George Karns is up for tenure too, right?" Rob seemed willing to face an uncomfortable possibility even if Claire wasn't.

"That's right," she answered reluctantly.

"Those notes aren't dated. Could this have happened five, maybe six years ago?" Rob's voice was tight with emotion.

"No, not if the initials are either Geraldine's or George's. The tenure decisions are made in the third year. Neither of them were on the faculty five or six years ago."

"Good. That's a relief," Rob sighed and relaxed back into the booth. The easy grin returned. Claire looked at the big man in surprise, and he attempted an explanation. "My mother died five years ago. She'd been sick a long time."

It took Claire a moment before Rob's meaning registered. He hadn't been as concerned about the possibility of his father's having had a homosexual lover as he was that the elder Rhodes had been unfaithful to his mother during her final illness.

"Whatever happened couldn't have occurred before her passing," Claire said softly. "So if that's why you showed me these notes, you have nothing to worry about on that score. But nothing here would seem to relate to your father's death."

"There's one more. See what you can make of this," he said pushing the final envelope across the table.

Claire opened the last note, and as she read, vitriol nearly dripped off the paper. Apparently Dr. Rhodes had let G. K. know that his support would not be forthcoming, and the writer responded with fury. The final sentence was particularly jarring, *"You, Judas! I ache to see you lying bleeding, dead at my feet!"*

Claire looked up at Rob, her green eyes huge. Whoever G. K. was, George or Geraldine, that person had just moved to the head of the list of murder suspects. The motive was clear: G. K. had expected tit for tat; the former, as it were, had been given, but latter had been denied—an outcome not taken lightly.

"Oh, Rob, you've got to show these to Captain Garrison, as soon as possible."

"I thought you'd say that," Rob remarked as he gathered up the seven notes and returned them to his jacket pocket. "But Garrison won't take kindly to me showing up. He and I knocked heads when we spoke earlier. I don't like the way he's running the investigation and let him know it. If I take these to him, he'll think I'm interfering."

"But you have to take them to him," Claire insisted.

"Not alone. I'd be too tempted to punch him out. I'll take them to him if you come along too. It'd be more difficult for either of us to flare up if a third party were present."

"Okay," Claire unwillingly agreed, "if you think my being there is necessary, I'll go. But I don't know why the two of you couldn't conduct yourselves like gentlemen; you both want the same thing: your father's murderer."

"That doesn't make me like the inept, arrogant cretin."

"All right, since the two of you can't play nice, I'll be there. I'm out of class at ten twenty tomorrow. I could meet you at his office then. He can sort out which G. K. it is."

"Thanks. I'd appreciate that. But I'm curious. Which one do you think it is?"

Claire thought a moment. Oftentimes one could tell by the penmanship if a writer had been a man or a woman, and she recalled the short, crisp, heavy strokes that made up the seven messages. But there was nothing in the notes' androgynous handwriting that, to her untrained eye, suggested the sex of G. K., so she based her judgment on, what seemed to her, the most obvious.

"Not George Karns, for sure. He's married and has a couple of kids."

"He wouldn't be the first man who was AC/DC."

Apparently what was obvious to Claire was not so straightforward to Rob, and that possibility caught her off guard.

"You're not troubled by what that would suggest about your father?" Claire asked surprised. That sort of behavior was not what she would have expected of the aloof and erudite Dr. Rhodes.

"I wasn't close to my father; besides, who knows what an aging, lonely man might be tempted to do. Maybe this Karns fellow didn't have much of a publication record either."

"I understand Karns' biggest problem is that he's on the technical writing staff. Most of the English faculty are literature teachers of one sort or another. Many think technical writing should be done away with."

"What about Geraldine Kosvoski? Is she in technical writing too?"

"No, world literature. But she was dating Sydney Andrews hot and heavy when the semester started, or so I've heard."

"Hot and heavy," Rob said thoughtfully. "*Was* dating?"

"Apparently Sydney dropped her sometime in late

September for the new departmental secretary, Sue Gooden."

"So in October and most of November Dr. Kosvoski was free to form other attachments. Perhaps she was somewhat free in her behavior too. Might she be a lady of easy virtue?" Rob asked, his intonation suggesting her virtue might bear examination.

"If she should be the one who wrote those notes, I'd rather characterize her as a lady of desperate virtue, trying to do whatever she could to hold on to her job in an unfriendly job market."

"Maybe I'll drop in on Geraldine Kosvoski tomorrow too," Rob said as the two left the booth heading for the cash register near the door. The glint in those blue eyes caused Claire to caution him.

"Go easy there. Geraldine may not be the one involved with your father; besides, she's had a rough enough time with Sydney. She deserves more than a quick roll in the hay."

The tall man grinned down at Claire knowingly. "How about a slow roll in the hay?" he asked.

Given his intense stare, Claire wasn't sure whether or not he was still talking about Geraldine.

As Claire and Rob stopped at the cashier's counter on the way to the door, they were unaware they were being watched by the gray-eyed police captain, who was sitting in an adjacent dining room. He recognized Rob Rhodes, and he frowned as he watched the exchange at the cashier's register. Claire tried to pay her bill, but the tall man beside her ignored her protests and laughingly took her check from her and paid the tab. Garrison's frown deepened as the two left together, talking earnestly. Through the front plate-glass window he watched them cross the parking lot, his frown darkening. The tall man stopped and opened the driver's door of a Ford Mustang. When Claire slipped behind the wheel and the tall man shut the door and stepped back, Garrison's frown began to fade. The frown was completely gone when the Mustang left the parking lot headed north and Rob Rhodes, hunched down in what must surely be a rental Toyota, left driving south.

Chapter Sixteen

The Tuesday morning meeting with Grant Garrison got off to a ragged start. Claire arrived at the captain's office before Rob, and she was embarrassed. This was the first time she had seen the officer since he told her the jacket had been found—with battery acid stains. Claire felt responsible for the trouble she had needlessly caused him.

"Captain Garrison, I want to tell you how sorry I am for mentioning that jacket to you. I feel horrible about the waste of time and effort it caused you," she said sincerely.

"Don't feel too bad; at least it gave the papers something positive to write about. They can't say our search isn't thorough. There wasn't an empty tin can or sour milk carton left unturned," he answered with a grin that was more nearly a grimace.

"I almost called to apologize but thought you probably didn't want to hear from the person who had caused you so much trouble," Claire explained.

"A few kind words are always appreciated." Garrison's grimace relaxed into a real smile. "Now. What sort of search are you about to send me on this time? According to your call, you have something to show me you think might relate to Dr. Rhodes' murder."

"Actually, I don't have it. It's something Rob Rhodes found while going through things at his father's house, some notes Dr. Rhodes had received. Rob should be here by now," she said, casting an anxious glance at the door.

"If he found it, in what way are you involved?" The smile disappeared.

"He didn't know whether or not it might be significant because he's unfamiliar with university procedures. He should be here any minute." Once more Claire looked toward the door uneasily. And once more she was wasting Captain Garrison's time. Fortunately she heard footsteps coming down the hall. "That's probably him now," she said, relieved. There was a sharp rap on the office door.

"Come in," Garrison called, and Rob entered, pulling himself up to full, impressive height.

Claire glanced quickly at the chest of Rob's tweed

jacket, looking for a telltale bulge. She saw none. Either he had left his gun at home or this jacket fit looser than the one he wore last night. Claire waited a moment, expecting him to produce the notes and explain where they were found, but Rob didn't. He stood glaring at Garrison. Claire looked back at the captain. He was on his feet glaring at Rob. It was a two-man stare down, and tension crackled between the two. Neither seemed willing to break eye contact. The hostile silence thickened until Claire felt forced to speak.

"Rob found seven notes that were written to his father by someone who only used the initials G. K."

She turned to Rob and held out her hand for the packet of notes. Never taking his eyes from Garrison, Rob slowly pulled them from his jacket pocket. Claire noted that this time he wasn't carrying the notes in the inside pocket. Maybe he was armed. Rob handed them to her, and she, in turn, passed them to Garrison, who took them without a glance, as cold gray and burning blue eyes continued the staring match. To her surprise, Rob reached out and proprietarily pulled her back away from Garrison.

Gently shrugging off his hand, Claire continued, since no one else seemed willing to say anything. "The notes seem to suggest a motive for murder, one that should be investigated." She bit her lip wondering if she were sending the captain on another wild goose chase. "When you read them, you'll see they are of a rather sensitive nature. I'm sure you'll be discreet in how you use them."

"Of course," Garrison responded tersely. "Anything else?"

Claire looked up at Rob questioningly, but he was still staring at Garrison, so she answered.

"No. I . . . we thought you ought to be aware of what's suggested in them, so we'll leave them with you now. Come on, Rob," she said, but it wasn't until she laid her hand on his arm that he broke his hard stare and looked down at her. Then he turned on his heel and ushered her toward the door.

"Good-bye, Captain Garrison," she called over her shoulder just as they entered the hallway.

But Captain Garrison didn't answer. His glare had turned to a scowl as he watched the couple walk away.

Back working at her desk in Morrill Hall, Claire laid a plastic bound research paper aside and posted a B+ in her gradebook. She sighed. Since returning from Garrison's office, she had only gotten one paper graded. If she didn't want to be snowed under with work when Dirk arrived, she needed to make a dent in the stack of folders before her. And today she was cutting her office hours short because she expected a call from him in the late afternoon. So when Elaine called to see if she was ready to go to lunch, Claire declined, saying she needed to keep working.

By the time she'd finished a second paper and picked up a third, her stomach was protesting and her concentration was wavering. No student should get a grade lower than deserved just because she was hungry and out of sorts, she decided. She could take care of both problems with a carryout sandwich from the cafeteria, and she left for a quick run to the Student Union.

As she stood in the pay-out line, she noticed a group of English faculty eating at a nearby table. Good, Claire thought. Elaine didn't have to eat alone. She had been joined by Geraldine Kosvoski, Lee Burrows, and David Stands. Claire would have been tempted to join them if it hadn't been for Sydney Andrews, whom she hadn't seen at first because he had been blocked from her view by Lee Burrows, the linguistics professor. Just as she reached the register to pay for her tuna sandwich and cup of coffee, George Karns and John North, a fellow technical writing professor, stopped at the crowded table on their way to the hall. Apparently George had something surprising to tell the group. When he finished, Elaine looked shocked, Lee disgusted, David doubtful, Sydney thoughtful, and Geraldine interested.

Although she was curious what George Karns had said, Claire knew she didn't have time to stop. Elaine would undoubtedly tell her later. Cutting through the seating area on her way to the hall, Claire waved to Elaine, and as she did, she overheard Lee Burrows exclaim indignantly, "Where does he think he is? The Wild West? Oklahoma's been a state for a hundred years!"

Claire's curiosity was pricked, but she hurried on. She had just reached the outside door when she heard a familiar voice call her name. Sydney had left the table and was following her. There was no point in trying to outrun him all the way back to Morrill Hall, so Claire waited for him to catch up.

"Did you know Rhodes' son is going around campus carrying a gun?" Sydney asked as he fell into step beside her.

Of course Claire knew, and she also knew why, but she had no intention of sharing that information with Sydney. Given the way his mind worked, he'd be asking her how she knew. Had she seen him without his jacket? Without his sweater? Without his slacks? So her response was brief and noncommittal.

"Really?" she answered with less interest than Sydney expected.

"Yeah. George Karns said Rhodes came to see him this morning, and he noticed the gun. Rhodes let his jacket gape open, and George thinks he intended for him to see it."

So she had been right. Rob did have a gun under that tweed sport coat when they met with Garrison, Claire thought, but she said, "Did he threaten George with it?"

"No. He didn't pull it out or anything. But Karns said he did feel threatened. And he didn't like the questions Rhodes asked him. Then Rhodes went to see Geraldine, but she said she was unaware of any gun."

"Well, if he deliberately let George see the gun, he surely has a permit to carry it," Claire commented.

"Maybe. Maybe not." Sydney seemed to be turning

something over in his mind before he added, "I wonder if Captain Garrison knows he's going around campus armed."

And I wonder if Captain Garrison knows Rob's going around asking questions of George Karns and Geraldine Kosvoski before he can, Claire thought.

Once more returned to her desk, Claire opened another research paper, and although she stared at the opening paragraph, she wasn't reading. Her mind was still on Rob Rhodes, a man with little tolerance for procedures and authority, an impatient man, a closed-mouthed man, at least as far as his own activities were concerned. She knew almost nothing about him. Oh, he could appear to be disarmingly candid on occasion, she thought, recalling their first conversation in her office and his reference to himself as the family black sheep, which suggested a rift between himself and his father, whom he had not seen for years. But perhaps he thought as little of the truth as he thought of Grant Garrison. How much of what he had told her was actually true? Maybe, while appearing to be honest, he'd dropped in a few well-placed lies to distance himself from Stillwater the night of his father's murder. He claimed to have met Dirk in Rome shortly before he got the word about his father. How short was "shortly"? Claire wondered. How rapidly could a person fly between Rome and Oklahoma City, make a quick trip by rental car to Stillwater in the dead of night, and then return to Italy? Might his own guilt be the reason he was trying so hard to pin the murder on someone else?

Suddenly Claire's cheeks blazed. But this time the red flush was aimed at herself, not at Rob Rhodes. Why was she trying so hard build a case against him? she asked herself, and she didn't like the answer. Might the fact that he was dangerously attractive be the reason she was willing to believe him capable of killing his father? Did believing that make it easier to hold him metaphorically at arm's length? The notion that she might be attracted to him was jarring, and Claire was disturbed at what it suggested about her. But now wasn't the time to deal with an examination of her character. Now was the time to get some serious grading done. Shaking off all other concerns, Claire focused on the research paper before her.

At three that afternoon Claire cut her office hours short. Taking a stack of ungraded papers with her, she left campus but not before getting a quick grapevine update from Elaine to share with Dirk when he called that afternoon. Well actually, because of the time difference, he'd call during his night and her late afternoon. The time differential continued to complicate their lives.

KayCee, her afternoon nap interrupted by Claire's early arrival, stood and with an insistent *meow* demanded to be petted. But Claire had no more than sat down with the cat on her lap when the phone rang, and she unceremoniously dumped the surprised animal in the floor as she hurried to the phone. This call promised to be a long one, and Claire had no intention of wasting a minute of it.

Dirk wanted a complete report on the murder investigation and an assurance that she was still not under suspicion.

"You're not trying to solve the murder yourself, are you?" he asked after Claire's update. "I know what you're like when you get on the trail of something you think is suspect," Dirk teased, referring to Claire's earlier activities when she was seeking to prove her dissertation thesis, activities that had meshed his life with hers.

His comment gave her a moment's pause. She hadn't stayed completely out of the investigation, she admitted to herself. She had passed on a couple of hints to Captain Garrison, and she hoped the note hint would be more productive than the jacket hint. Briefly she considered not mentioning that slight involvement to Dirk. He was worried enough about her. Yet, not to mention it was sort of lying by omission, and it was important for them to be honest with each other. She began by trying to reassure him.

"As I told you, I'm happy to report that, as far as the campus police are concerned, I'm no longer among the possible guilty, but others in the department haven't been so fortunate."

"What do you mean 'others in the department haven't

been so fortunate'?" Dirk asked sharply, sensing she had been more involved than she was letting on.

Claire downplayed her role regarding the notes Dr. Rhodes' son had shown her and had taken to the police—notes that moved two fellow professors, both with the initials G. K., to the top of Garrison's list. Grant Garrison interviewed them, Elaine Evans had told her, but Rob Rhodes had gotten to them first, much to Garrison's increasing anger, and, both Geraldine Kosvoski and George Karns were now hiring lawyers.

"Elaine said Captain Garrison is really ticked off at Rhodes' interference. Oh yes! Speaking of Rob Rhodes—would you believe it? You've met him! He knows your director, Richard Steele, and visited your set."

"Now that you mention it, there was a fellow named Rhodes here, a big guy. Robert, I believe, Richard called him. He spent the day at the set and then we all went to dinner together. That would have been the Tuesday before Thanksgiving, just shortly before you e-mailed me about Dr. Rhodes' death, in fact. I hadn't connected the two."

"Rob's the youngest son." And he's an innocent son too, Claire realized. Tuesday in Rome would have over-lapped with Monday in Stillwater. No matter how fast jets flew there hadn't been time for him to make a quick roundtrip to Oklahoma to stab his father. Thank heaven she hadn't mentioned that suspicion to Garrison.

"Are you sure it's the same person? The fellow I met was huge, two or three inches taller than I, well-built. But what I remember the most about him was his eyes. They were the most vivid, intensely blue eyes I've ever seen."

"That sounds just like Dr. Rhodes' son."

"Does it? And I also remember something else—his reciprocated appreciation of the ladies," Dirk tacked on uneasily. "How well do you know this guy?"

Claire detected a slightly worried tone in Dirk's question.

"Not at all, actually."

"Then why did he show you the notes he found?"

That was the same question Grant Garrison had asked her, and she gave the same answer. He just needed to ask someone who was familiar with college procedures if they might be significant.

"But he asked you rather than someone else." That was a statement, not a question, and not a very happy statement at that.

"He'd been to see me. He's visited with everyone who had been connected in some way with his father. As far as knowing him is concerned, as I said, I don't. He's very reticent about who he is and what he does. All he'll admit to is being the family black sheep."

"He may be a black sheep, but he's the kind of man who draws women like honey draws flies," Dirk said, falling back on a tired cliché. "One should always be careful around black sheep, Claire," Dirk warned.

"I'm not a fly and I'm not interested in sheep of any color." And as she spoke Claire knew she was speaking the truth. She might be intrigued by Rob, but she loved Dirk. "I'm only interested in one rather handsome actor, who can't get back to the States fast enough to suit me!"

And their conversation shifted to warm topics other than dead professors and tall, blue-eyed men. After they had finally hung up, Claire sat lost in thought. Although she tried to deny it to herself, she couldn't help but worry about Dirk and the beautiful women he was surrounded with in Italy, especially since Jill Tyler, his ex-fiancée, was in Rome. Then she smiled slowly. Maybe it was all right if he was just a little bit concerned about the temptations she might face in his absence.

Chapter Seventeen

Early Wednesday morning both Claire's alarm clock and telephone starting ringing at the same time. Blindly she turned off the alarm and groped for the phone. Trying not to sound as sleepy as she felt, she answered it and was surprised the caller was Rob.

"Do I have you to thank for being hauled into Garrison's office last night?" he asked. Fortunately she detected a trace of humor in his voice.

"Hauled into Garrison's office? No, that wasn't me. You probably have yourself to thank for that. I understand he wasn't happy you'd already talked to Geraldine and George."

"That did come up during the interrogation," the big man acknowledged, "but the reason I got pulled in was because of my gun."

160

"And that wasn't me either. Although Karns said he'd seen it and was talking about it in the Union yesterday. Said you'd deliberately let him see the gun, and he felt threatened."

"He must frighten easily then. So the word's out that I'm armed, huh?"

"I'm afraid so. And any number of people might have complained to Captain Garrison."

"If I knew who, I might know who's trying to break in here. And if I knew that, I might also know who killed Dad." Rob Rhodes no longer sounded mildly amused.

"Did the prowler come back a third time?" Claire exclaimed.

"Yeah. While I was tied up at Garrison's office, someone went to work on the patio door again—cracked the glass this time, dented the door frame even worse, but the lock held. I don't know if I scared him off when I pulled into the driveway or if he'd already given up and left, but whoever it was didn't get in."

"Since the word is out you're armed, maybe that will discourage the prowler. You are still armed, aren't you?"

"Right. I told you I had a permit, remember?"

"I remember. What did Garrison say about your seeing Geraldine and George before he could?"

"The short version is that while I have a license for the gun, I have no license to interfere with a police investigation. The only reason he didn't cite me was because of how it would look."

"How it would look? Did he say that?"

"Not in so many words, but that's what he meant. As you know, his department has had a lot of bad publicity regarding the investigation, and arresting the son of the murder victim wouldn't play well in the press, especially when all the son's trying to do is find his father's killer since the police aren't able to."

"So he let you off with a warning?"

"A warning that lasted almost two hours, enough time for someone to make another break-in attempt."

"And that someone could be either George Karns or Geraldine Kosvoski. When you talked with them yesterday, what did they say? Could you figure out which one wrote the notes?"

"No, not yet, but the conversations were interesting. However, you don't have time for me to go into all that right now. You need to get ready for class. I'll talk with you later." And Rob hung up.

Claire stood in the shower, letting the warm water sluice over her. She was aware of the strange connection between warm water and her brain. She got her best ideas for papers and lesson plans while standing in the shower, almost as if the warm water loosened up her thought processes. This morning she wasn't thinking about papers or lesson plans. Because of Rob's early call, she was thinking about Dr. Rhodes' murderer, who was still at large and who, apparently, was still searching for something he believed Rhodes had. Since the briefcase was held by the police and unavailable, the murderer had thrice tried to break into the Rhodes' home. Claire shuddered to think what might happen should that person encounter Rob Rhodes and the handgun he carried under his left arm.

Because of the notes she and Rob had taken to Garrison, notes that supplied a motive for the murder, suspicion now fell on either Geraldine Kosvoski or George Karns. But the more she thought about it the more difficulty Claire had in believing either of them were guilty. George had never struck her in the slightest way of being attracted to men, which left Geraldine. True, Geraldine had no alibi, and, if the notes were hers, she would have had reason to be furious with Rhodes, but that did not necessarily mean she had acted on her fury. In the heat of the moment angry women say a lot of things they'd never act on.

As Claire turned to let the warm water course down her back, her thoughts focused on Rhodes' briefcase. That case must hold some sort of clue, she reasoned, or at least the murderer feared it did because it was all that was taken from Rhodes' office. Claire recalled what Grant had told her. The killer had been looking for something when he was surprised by Dr. Rhodes. In his haste to leave the office, he took the briefcase, hoping what he wanted was in it. Perhaps it wasn't, and that was why he was trying to get into Rhodes' home to search there. Yet, if he'd checked the briefcase, why did he need to hide it? Claire wondered. Hiding it suggested he intended to return for it.

The only thing in that briefcase that seemed out of place was the Faulkner paper, which had been written by some fellow totally unrelated to anyone on campus. Maybe that was it, Claire thought eagerly; maybe the killer wasn't anyone on campus. But as quickly as that thought came, it faded. The killer apparently had a master key to the English offices, which had been taken from a former secretary's desk. No out-of-towner would have known about the existence of the key, let alone been able to find it and take it. So who did know about the key? Not the current department secretary. That had already been established. People who had been around since the days of Dr. McMichaels might have. The former secretary, Phyllis Whitman, had only a faint memory of it. Dr. Millington certainly knew about the duplicate key, of course. And Claire supposed he might have taken it sometime over the years, but if he had, then why had he mentioned it that morning in the Union? Besides, he had no more reason to kill Rhodes than she had.

Claire turned off the faucets and reached for a towel. The Faulkner paper nagged at her. Why would an Elizabethan and Jacobean scholar be carrying a paper about William Faulkner, no matter who it was written by? There was only one answer: It had been sent to him as the editor of *The Oracle*. He probably intended to read it before he sent it on to the others on the review board. That was the only logical reason for Dr. Rhodes to have such a paper with him. And Claire should have been satisfied with that answer, but as she toweled off, she wasn't. Surely if he had received one submission, he had received more, but it was just the Faulkner paper he was carrying. Because it seemed too oddly out of place, she was sure that paper had to be key to Dr. Rhodes' murder.

The more she thought about that paper, the more familiar the notion behind the title "Flem Snopes: American Everyman" seemed to be. She'd seen a similar article somewhere. The notion teased her enough that she decided to try to track it down the next time she had a spare moment. Spare moments were hard to come by. Tests and research papers were waiting to be graded. Dirk was scheduled to fly into Oklahoma City the Wednesday of finals week, and she was determined not be bogged down with school work when he arrived. They hadn't been together since mid-August.

Finally, on Thursday afternoon after hours of steady grading, Claire's head needed a break. She laid her red pen aside and stretched. In an effort to get her blood circulating, she walked down the hall to the main office to see if the afternoon mail had arrived. It hadn't, or if it had, it hadn't been sorted yet, and the secretary, busy typing, ignored Claire. Claire was about to return to her waiting papers when she noticed the bookcases across the office from the secretary's desk. Shelved there were back issues of several English journals available for faculty and student use. Not quite ready to resume work, Claire decided maybe this was as good a time as any to look for the Faulkner article that was bothering her, and she walked to the bookshelves.

"Can I help you with something?" Sue Gooden snapped, looking up from the test she was entering into the computer and scowling as Claire seated herself before the row of journals and began pulling them off the shelf one at a time to check the tables of contents.

"No thanks, I'm just trying to run something down," Claire responded mildly to Sue's sharp tone.

"Well, those journals are in chronological order," Sue snipped.

"I see that."

"So be sure you put them back like you found them." Sue's tone suggested that Claire had no business looking through those journals.

Claire looked at the secretary evenly. "Aren't these here for faculty use?"

"I suppose. If you take any, be sure you sign for them. There's a clipboard on the bottom shelf," Sue ordered. With that the secretary continued her typing, pounding the keys with more vigor than required. Waves of dislike or disapproval or downright hostility radiated off Sue Gooden and, from her frequent use of the Delete key, affected her typing.

You ought to save that attitude for someone who's after Sydney Andrews, Claire thought. But she said nothing and reached for another journal. She found articles about Faulkner, but by their titles, none of them dealt with the Snopeses. *This is probably just a waste of time,* she thought with a grimace, *but not as unpleasant as sifting through the city dump.* She was still feeling guilty about what she had put Grant Garrison and his men through.

The collection of journals finished with issues of *The Oracle,* the quarterly publication Dr. Rhodes was about to edit and the journal Sydney Andrews had been published in. *Lucky Andrews!* she thought as she opened the first journal. The last year's quarterlies contained no Faulkner articles. With a sigh of frustration, she opened the spring issue of *The Oracle* for the preceding year. Her eye skimmed down the table of contents and halted on the title "Flem Snopes: A Twenty-first-Century American." She hadn't been imagining things; she had found it! More than finding the article that had eluded her, she had also found Sydney Andrews' article. He had written it. Talk about a coincidence! Although it had been her intention only to scan the article quickly, Claire decided since it had been written by a colleague, she'd check the journal out and read it more carefully. As Claire signed for the journal on the clipboard checkout sheet, her eyes ran up the list of signatures above hers. There on the third line from the top was Geraldine Kosvoski's name. Claire caught her breath. The capital G and K were signed with the same distinctive backward slant she had seen on the incriminating notes. No homosexual relationship had been involved. George Karns was straight, and Geraldine was in trouble. Claire was about to return the clipboard to the shelf when Sue Gooden spoke so pleasantly Claire turned around in surprise.

"Good afternoon. Is there anything you'd like me to do for you, Dr. Andrews?"

Claire heard a suggestive lilt in Sue's voice. If honey could have dripped from spoken words, Sydney would have been sticky. The secretary was smiling charmingly at the professor.

"Not right now, Sue." Then ignoring the eager young woman and turning to Claire, he said, "So there you are; I just stopped by your office. Thought you might be ready for a Coke, but here you are looking at journals." He took the clipboard from her and looked at what she had just written. "Ah, an issue of *The Oracle.* That's the one my article is in."

Claire would have been just as happy if Sydney Andrews didn't know she was interested in what he had written. But she could think of no quick way to hide her intention.

"Yes. I just found it. I've known so few people who have been published in that particular journal, I thought I'd read your article. And I've always enjoyed Faulkner. Your take on that character sounds interesting."

"Actually, it was something I knocked out in a bit of a hurry," Sydney said deprecatively. "I sent it to *The Oracle* more for their critiques than with the expectation of getting it published. Needless to say, their acceptance of it was a nice surprise. Now, how about that Coke?"

He was about to take her elbow. From the corner of her eye, Claire could see Sue's face, and the redhead was furious. Geraldine had said she and Sydney had been dating earlier in the year, and the young secretary was clearly chafing at being so openly ignored while her former boyfriend asked another woman out right in front of her. Claire, deftly sidestepping Sydney's grasp, wasn't sure what she disliked the most: Sydney's persistence when she was obviously not interested or his blatant disregard for Sue's feelings.

"Thanks, but I think not. I should get back to my grading, and I need to get home. I'm expecting a call from Dirk," she said, knowing she had used that excuse before but hoping he'd finally take the hint and find someone else to ask out for Cokes.

Sydney wasn't discouraged. "Well, when you finish my article, let me know. I'm interested in what you think of it. Maybe we could talk about it over dinner."

You just don't give up, do you? Claire said to herself. But to him she said as politely as she was able, "That sounds awfully like a date, and I'm engaged. I supposed you knew that."

Sydney lifted an eyebrow. "But you went out with Rob Rhodes, didn't you? I saw the two of you leaving that restaurant Monday night."

"That wasn't a date!" Claire protested. "I just met him there."

"Sure you did," Sydney snidely agreed. "Honey, I can do better than a pancake at IHOP. Think about it."

He was still smirking as she grabbed the journal and hurried from the office, leaving the field to Sue. Claire's cheeks burned. She was furious. Her supper with Rob was not a date, she fumed, although it might have looked like it to anyone who passed by, as Sydney apparently had. And she was angry Sydney had caught her with that journal. As conceited as he was, he'd probably take her interest in his article as an interest in him.

Chapter Eighteen

To be honest with herself, Claire actually was interested in Sydney, although not in the way he obviously hoped. Her interest in him went no further than his article, which she was eager to read. She was also eager to tell both Rob and Captain Garrison who the G. K. was that had signed the notes to Dr. Rhodes. As soon as she reached her office, she first called Captain Garrison, but the receptionist said he was unavailable at the moment. *He's probably interviewing either Geraldine or George*, Claire thought and declined the offer to leave a message. She was also unable to reach Rob. His ringing phone went unanswered. Apparently Dr. Rhodes had no answering machine. Disappointed she couldn't share what she had learned, Claire picked up a stack of ungraded tests and left for her apartment.

Shortly before five she tried calling both men again. Once more the captain wasn't available and Rob wasn't answering. Claire hung up the phone, flipped on the TV for the evening news, and stalked into the kitchen, KayCee at her heels meowing for supper.

"By this time Garrison's probably already figured out who G. K. is anyway," Claire muttered to herself as she poured dry cat food into KayCee's bowl. "But I doubt he'll hurry to tell Rob. What is it with those two, KayCee?" she asked the calico, who was too busy eating to pay any attention to her.

After a quick supper of her own and a slow conversation with Dirk, she tried Rob's number again. She was sure if Garrison had figured out the initials, he wouldn't willingly or rapidly inform Rob. And for the third time, there was no answer. Claire frowned as she hung up the phone. Where could he be? she wondered. She hoped Grant Garrison hadn't found another reason to run him in, but that was their business. Right now she was interested in Sydney's article, and she picked up the journal, settled on the divan, and began to read. Forty-five minutes later she thoughtfully closed the journal. KayCee, feeling ignored, jumped onto her lap, once more nosing under her hand for attention. Claire absently stroked the purring cat with the contentedly kneading front paws as she considered Andrews' article on Flem Snopes.

She was right. She had read that article when she was in graduate school, but at that time the name Sydney Andrews meant nothing to her. It was a surprisingly good article; no wonder she had remembered it. Sydney's sensitivity to fictional characters was much keener than his sensitivity to real people, Claire noted, recalling his abrupt behavior to Sue that afternoon. His article was so good Haskell Billingham, whoever he was, must have been motivated by it.

"Yeah, who is Haskell Billingham anyway, I wonder?" Claire murmured under her breath as she set the cat aside and went to her desk to boot up her computer. She clicked on Safari on her iMac, and she Googled "Haskell Billingham." There she found a number of Billinghams and Bellinghams and Haskells but no Haskell Billingham.

"Well, drat! First I can't talk with Garrison or Rob, and now I can't find out anything about Haskell Billingham. Guess that's par for the course," she grumbled as she put the Apple on "Sleep." Still the article weighed on her mind. She wondered how similar the two papers might be. The titles were certainly similar: "Flem Snopes: A Twenty-first-Century American," and, what did Grant say was the title of the paper in Dr. Rhodes' briefcase? It was something like "Flem Snopes: American Everyman." Could the Billingham person have borrowed from Andrews, maybe even plagiarized? Claire frowned at that thought. She was familiar with plagiarism. It has been the subject of her dissertation. But surely if Billingham had borrowed freely from Sydney's published paper, he wouldn't have had the nerve to submit it to the same journal that had published the original article. But if this paper wasn't a submission, what was Dr. Rhodes doing with it?

Was the similarity in titles something she should call to Garrison's attention? Claire wondered. She started to reach for the phone but stopped before she picked it up. He was busy. Besides, he wouldn't be interested in her ideas, not after the jacket fiasco. That had caused him to lose valuable time and probably his credibility too, with the OSBI. Next she had steered him onto the writer of the seven incriminating notes written, she was certain, by Geraldine Kosvoski. But according to this evening's news, no arrest had been made even though newspaper editorials were still criticizing the captain roundly for lack of progress in the case. Garrison must feel he didn't have a solid enough case against Geraldine. *Perhaps he has reason to be cautious of my information,* Claire thought. *What's the saying? Once bitten, twice shy. Have I given him too many red herrings to chase?* No, she wouldn't add to his problems more than she already had, she decided firmly. Besides, she had her own problems to deal with, and she lay *The Oracle* aside, picked up her red pen, and reached for another ungraded test. She'd call Rob later about those initials, and she wouldn't call Grant Garrison at all.

Claire had more problems than she knew. A dark blue Saturn was parked in the shadows across the street from her apartment building, and in that car sat a figure in a brown jacket watching her lit window.

I guess Garrison's not going to do anything with those notes I've sent him about Markham. But if the OSBI had the case, what would they make of her? She's too nosey for her own good. She needs to be stopped. I wonder if she knows what curiosity did to the cat?

Two hours later with a huge sign of relief, Claire finished the last test. She'd be able to return them tomorrow, so her American Novel students could see where they stood gradewise before going into finals. She still had a few research papers to finish, and, of course, she would have three sets of final tests to grade next week. Next week! That's when Dirk would be back. Thoughts of that meeting were interrupted by the ringing of the phone. *Who could that be?* she wondered. She and Dirk had already talked today, and it was after ten. Probably it was one of the three students who had yet to turn in a research paper with a pitiful plea for more time. But the male voice on the line was not a student; it was Rob Rhodes.

"Rob! I'm glad you called. I've been trying to reach you," she said eagerly.

"Really?" He sounded pleased. "Let me give you my cell numb—"

Claire in her excitement overrode him. "I know who G. K. is! It's Geraldine Kosvoski. I saw her signature. The *G* and *K* were written with that same backward slant that's on those notes."

"And have you told Garrison?" he asked sharply.

"No. I haven't been able to reach him, but he's probably already figured it out. I thought you should know."

"Thanks, but Geraldine's already told me the notes were hers. She also said that although she had been mad enough to kill Dad, she didn't."

"She told you that?" Claire exclaimed. "Do you believe her?"

"I do."

"Why?"

"Oklahoma has capital punishment, doesn't it?"

"Well . . . yes, it does. By lethal injection."

"Then I think she's innocent because it'd be a crime to waste that much woman."

"Maybe so. But I doubt that defense would hold up in court."

"You're probably right. But I spoke with her before Garrison got there and let her know what to expect."

"And you deserved that dressing down you got from him. Interfering with a police investigation isn't the behavior one would expect of a man who's trying to find his father's killer."

"Unless that man has stumbled onto something else. I've found some more letters here at Dad's I'd like to show you if it's not too late."

"Are they from people on campus?" Claire inquired.

"Not according to the letterheads."

Claire glanced at her watch. Rob was right, it was late, but if he'd found something that shifted the onus from

Geraldine and anyone on campus, Claire would gladly help.

"Sure. Come on over. Do you know where I live?"

"Dad had all the addresses of the English faculty on his Rolodex. I'll be there in ten minutes."

Rob got there in eight minutes, and the two made themselves comfortable on the couch with the letters he wanted her to see.

"These may mean nothing, but I thought someone else should check them before they go into the shredder," he said, handing her five envelopes.

"That someone really should be Grant Garrison, not me," Claire remarked as she opened the top envelope.

The vivid blue eyes gleamed mischievously. "Why would I want to spend time with Garrison when I could be with you?"

Claire ignored the implied compliment, although it was difficult. Those blue eyes were almost hypnotic, and he was sitting closer than she had realized. She forced her attention on the first letter and read it carefully.

"I don't see anything really suspect in this. The fellow—a Dr. James Cardwell," she said, glancing at the signature, "is put out because your father won't collaborate on a book. The return address is Charlottesville, Virginia. That's a long way to go to kill someone in a fit of pique because he won't coauthor a book."

Claire continued through the letters. Two were angry responses from professors who felt his harsh criticism of their papers at a Modern Language Association convention was unprofessional. The fourth was from an unsuccessful litigator who believed he'd been treated unfairly when the court settled in Dr. Rhodes' favor. The last letter concerned a complaint from a former colleague regarding an unfavorable recommendation he believed Dr. Rhodes had written, when he was applying for another position.

"Rob, I think it would really be stretching it to think any of these people were angry enough at your father to kill him." A thought suddenly occurred to her. "You haven't found a letter from a Haskell Billingham, have you?"

"No."

"Are you sure?"

"That's an odd name. I'd have remembered it if I had; however, I'm not quite finished going through things. If I find something by him, do you want me to show it to you?"

"Yes, please, because—"

Claire stopped in midsentence. She felt warm breath on her cheek and a large, warm hand on her thigh. His free hand curled behind her head and gently began rubbing her neck below her left ear. His mouth was dangerously near hers. She was so surprised it took her a moment to react, and in that moment she realized Rob knew as well as she that these letters in no way related to his father's murder, that they had just been an excuse for him to be alone with her.

"Move your hand," she said more firmly than she felt. It would have been so easy not to have spoken at all. Suddenly Rob Rhodes looked like honey and she knew how flies felt. The hard wall of his chest pressed seductively against her shoulder. He wasn't wearing his side arm tonight.

Rob did as asked. He moved his hand. The large, warm hand slid higher on her thigh and slipped toward the inside.

Claire stiffened. What was she doing?! She'd never been unfaithful during a relationship in her life, and she had no intention of starting now—no matter what she feared Dirk might be doing in Italy. Not willingly! But there was no way she could overpower the big man or even get from the couch if he decided to keep her there.

"Take you hands off me right now, and get out!" she said forcefully, trying to pull away, but the hand behind her head held her in place.

Rob leaned closer; his hand tightened on her thigh and his lips brushed her cheek.

"Are you sure?" he whispered softly.

"I couldn't be any more sure! Get out!" she hissed, arching her back and trying once more to twist from his grasp.

To her surprise, the big man grinned suddenly and sat back, taking his hands with him.

"Can't blame me for trying." He stooped to pick up the letters Claire had dropped in her surprise and rose, smiling at her once again. Claire, who had scrambled to her feet, put the coffee table between him and herself. "You're clearly not interested, and I've never forced a woman in my life."

Claire believed him. With those hypnotic blue eyes, he wouldn't need force. Women would melt willingly into his strong arms.

"However, I am both sorry and glad," he added with a rueful shrug.

"Sorry and glad?" Claire asked, looking up at him confused.

"Yes. Sorry for me. You're a most attractive woman, Claire Markham. But I'm glad for Dirk. The man's been living like a monk. I'm glad his restraint has been worth it." And with a half salute with the letters he carried, he turned toward the door.

"Rob."

The big man stopped with his hand on the doorknob.

"Thank you for telling me," Claire called softly.

"I thought you'd like to know," he answered, and then he was gone.

Chapter Nineteen

Claire's Friday classes were review sessions, as Thursday's had been. Finals week would begin on Monday, and she wanted her students to do well. After a quick lunch in the Union with Elaine, she was back at her desk going over the notes for her last class of the semester when her phone rang.

"Claire, it's me, Rob. Don't hang up. I was out of line last night. I know that. I hope we can still be friends."

His voice was so apologetic and contrite Claire couldn't even pretend to be angry.

"So long as you know that's all we'll ever be. So what's up? Not another break-in attempt, I hope?"

"No, not since the night Garrison pulled me in and kept me there so long. Things have been quiet since then.

181

I guess word is out that I'm prepared for impromptu company."

"Have you found something from Haskell Billingham?" Claire asked eagerly.

"No, I'm afraid not. I haven't had time to start looking again. But since you'd seen those notes from Geraldine, I thought you'd be interested to know that although she wrote them, she didn't kill Dad."

"So you said yesterday. And I'd be happy to believe her too, but how can you be so sure? She doesn't have an alibi for that night."

"Oh, yes, she does. It was just one she hoped she wouldn't have to use, but then Garrison started leaning on her about those notes that appeared to give her a motive. I finally convinced her to tell Garrison. She's in his office right now."

"But she's already said she was alone, that there was no one who could vouch for her presence."

"She lied. She spent the night with Lee Burrows. His wife thought he was at a conference in Dallas."

"Really." The news surprised but didn't shock Claire. She had suspected Burrows had a roving eye; however, his wife had always seemed to keep him on a short leash. "And will he back her up?"

"He reluctantly offered to before, but she thought the killer would be found, and she wouldn't have to blow his cover. He's at Garrison's office with her." Rob sounded relieved.

"And will Garrison believe them?"

"I'd think so. Granted, Geraldine lied to him earlier, but it's an understandable lie. She was trying to protect a married lover as long as possible. And the fact that Burrows is there to back up her story should be convincing. A married family man wouldn't lie about something like that just to help out a friend, not if it could mean his marriage."

"I'm surprised Burrows had that much backbone."

"Well, I'll have to admit, I might have helped stiffen it a bit this morning," Rob chuckled.

"Really? He didn't just 'accidentally' get a glimpse of that gun you carry, did he?" Maybe Rob didn't force women to comply, but perhaps that delicacy didn't extend to his dealings with men.

"If he did, it was an accident," Rob answered. "No. I just reminded him in my best persuasive manner that while Geraldine hadn't told his wife about their tryst, I would. However, if he volunteered that information to Garrison, the captain might be able to keep it quiet as would I." Rob paused, apparently realizing he had just given lie to that promise. "Well, I guess I am telling you, aren't I?"

"And it will go no farther. I have no reason to embarrass neither him nor Geraldine."

"Good. And I can attest to the fact you can be trusted," Rob answered, alluding, Claire knew, to what had transpired on her couch the night before. "Anyway, I suggested to Burrows that his only hope of keeping his wife ignorant of his activities would be to confide in

Garrison and trust in his discretion. And, as I said, he and Geraldine are seeing Garrison now."

It was Claire's turn to chuckle. "Rob, you're an odd person. You're impatient with Garrison and criticize him for being so slow in finding your father's killer, yet you help a suspect establish an alibi."

"That's not so odd. I want the right person found and punished. Geraldine Kosvoski isn't the right person, but she is a very interesting person. I like her more every time I see her."

Claire briefly considered asking him if he wasn't troubled that a woman would move so quickly from Sydney Andrews to his father to Lee Burrows, but instead she said, "And the last time you saw her was—"

"After I left your apartment last night."

Claire blinked. Geraldine wasn't the only person who moved fast, she realized.

"As I was driving back to the house, I started thinking about that last note she wrote. A woman with that much fire and passion shouldn't be locked up just to keep Lee Burrows out of trouble with his wife."

"But you didn't know about Lee Burrows then."

"True, but I did know she shouldn't be jailed."

"So you talked with her, she told you about Burrows, and you convinced her it was time for her to quit protecting him." Claire couldn't resist adding, "Were you able to convince her of anything else?"

"Ah. That would be telling, wouldn't it? But there's

no woman quite like a robust woman." Rob was laughing at Claire's answering snort when she hung up.

Claire sank back into her desk chair, digesting what she had just learned. So Geraldine Kosvoski was innocent of murder, and Lee Burrows was an adulterer. She was glad about Geraldine and indifferent to Burrows, but she was concerned about what this meant for Grant Garrison. Once more she had pointed him at a potential murderer and sent him on a fruitless chase. He was no closer to solving Dr. Rhodes' murder than he was the day it happened—maybe even further away. Time was passing, the trail was growing colder, and every possible lead had turned up a blank.

That afternoon Claire quite literally ran into the man she was concerned about. She had stopped in the central English office to check her mailbox. In it she found two Christmas cards from grad school friends and the three missing research papers, obviously put there by students who knew they were late and didn't want to face their professor. Grant Garrison was leaving Dr. Larkin's office as Claire turned from the mail pigeon holes with her hands full. Garrison was hurried and preoccupied, and Claire was concentrating on how much to penalize the late papers when the two collided.

"Sorry about that," the OSU police captain said as he bent to pick up the cards and papers he had knocked to the floor.

"No problem. Actually, I'm the one who should be apologizing."

"Why? I didn't drop anything."

"Because of what I told you about those notes," Claire said softly, aware Sue Gooden had seen them collide and was trying to listen.

"So you've already heard about my interview this afternoon. I suppose Rob Rhodes told you."

"Yes. He called me. I trust you believe what was said?" Claire was deliberately being oblique. Sue was straining to hear.

"I'd be hard-pressed not to, given the circumstances. So, what else do you have for me? Any more ideas?"

Claire was grateful he hadn't said "Any more bright ideas?"

"No. Well, actually . . . it's not an idea, really; it's more just an observation."

"Which is?"

"Do you really want to know? I'm sure it doesn't mean anything. Nothing else I've told you about has."

"At this point, I'll listen to anything."

"Okay, then. What was the name again of that Faulkner paper you found in Dr. Rhodes' briefcase?"

Garrison frowned, thinking. "It was something like 'Somebody Snopes: Everyman's American.' No, that doesn't sound right." The frown deepened.

" 'Flem Snopes: American Everyman?' " Claire corrected hopefully.

"Yeah, that's right. 'Flem Snopes: American Everyman.' Sorry. I majored in political science, not American literature."

"The reason I asked was because year before last, Sydney Andrews had an article published entitled 'Flem Snopes: A Twenty-first-Century American.' I was struck with the similarities between those two titles. I found Andrews' article yesterday and read it."

"And?"

"And it's very good. Excellent, in fact. I'd be interested to know if the fellow who wrote the paper you found had been influenced by the Andrews' article. And if so, to what extent."

"But even if Billingham had copied it word for word, how does that relate to Dr. Rhodes' murder?"

"I don't know. It probably doesn't. That's why I said it was an observation not an idea, which is why I was hesitant to mention it. But I'm curious. I'd surely like to see Billingham's paper," Claire said, looking up hopefully at Grant Garrison as the two walked out of the English office together.

Sue Gooden waited until the two cleared the door, and then she reached for the phone.

As they walked toward Claire's office, Garrison asked, "Do you still have that article by Andrews?"

"Yes. The journal's at my apartment."

Garrison didn't say anything for a moment. He obviously was considering something before he spoke.

"You understand I can't turn Billingham's paper over to you. I'd have to be there when you read it."

"Of course. Are you saying you're going to let me see it?" Claire asked eagerly.

"Maybe. I'll consider it."

And with a nod, he left her at her office door.

Chapter Twenty

That evening Claire began a major cleaning of her apartment in preparation for Dirk's Wednesday arrival. While she was changing KayCee's litter box under the watchful eye of the large cat, the phone rang.

"Dr. Markham. It's Grant Garrison. If you're still interested, you can see that paper we talked about," he said brusquely.

"Yes, I'm still interested. When?" she asked eagerly.

"Tonight? I could meet you at your office in half an hour."

"That would be great!" House-cleaning was a task she was always happy to put off. Besides, if Garrison was willing to let her see Billingham's paper, she'd better do it before he changed his mind. "I'm really curious

189

how similar the two are. I'll bring the journal so we can compare them."

"All right. I'll see you in thirty minutes, then," he replied.

"Right. And thanks!" she said before hanging up.

Claire took time to finish the litter box chore. If she didn't, she knew KayCee would likely use the kitchen floor to signal her disapproval that her needs hadn't been attended to. She'd finish the rest of the cleaning tomorrow, she decided as she washed her hands. Although she didn't have time for a shower, she did have time to change into a fresh sweatshirt. Fortunately, this time there was a clean one in the closet that didn't have frayed cuffs and a hole by the neck band, but on a whim she passed it over for a yellow long-sleeved turtleneck sweater. Shirt changed, she made a quick pass with the hair brush and dabbed on a little lipstick before slipping into her jacket and winding the long green scarf around her neck. Picking up the copy of *The Oracle*, she hurried to the door. Garrison's call had surprised her. There was no real reason for letting her see Billingham's paper. There was no way a submission to *The Oracle* could be connected to Dr. Rhodes' murder. Garrison must really be desperate, she thought as she drove to the campus.

"Okay. So he's desperate, and I'm curious," Claire murmured under her breath as she pulled into a parking slot in the nearly empty Morrill Hall lot. Just as she entered the east door of the building, a second car, a dark blue Saturn, parked at the west end of the same lot and a figure in a brown leather jacket got out, also headed for Morrill Hall.

Claire, waiting in her office, checked her watch. She was a little early, and she hoped Garrison wouldn't be late. She was uneasy being alone in the dark, old building. Working here at night had never bothered her before, but she hadn't been here this late since Dr. Rhodes had been murdered, and that realization sent a flood of goose pimples racing down her spine. "Hurry up, Garrison," she whispered as she opened the journal to Sydney's article in preparation for his arrival. Exactly thirty minutes after he had called her apartment there was a knock on her office door. The gray-eyed police officer had arrived, and in his hand he held, not Dr. Rhodes' briefcase, but a manila file folder.

"Here it is," he said, handing her the folder.

"And I've got Andrews' article here on my desk. Make yourself comfortable. You can hang your jacket over there, if you like, and pull up a chair," she said, gesturing to the coat tree in the corner and the chairs before the fireplace as she returned to her desk. "Here's the article," she said, handing him the journal as the two sat down to work.

Claire opened the folder. The paper inside wasn't what she expected. The format didn't look like that of a journal submission. There was no cover sheet nor page headers, and the pages had been stapled at the left corner.

"Oops. Looks like Billingham didn't follow the MLA style sheet. That won't impress the review team," she commented, flipping through the pages. "In fact, this looks more like a term paper."

"Check the last page," Garrison said.

Claire did. There in red ink she found a large *A* with a triple plus sign and a lengthy paragraph of praise written by some former professor. She looked up at Garrison frowning in confusion.

"Then this wasn't a journal submission. It was a term paper."

"It looks that way to me," Garrison agreed.

"But Dr. Rhodes had no student named Haskell Billingham, right? So what was he doing with this?"

"That was what I was hoping you could help me with. But first, let's compare the two."

"What would be the best way to do this, do you think?" Claire asked.

"How about if we take turns reading aloud paragraph by paragraph? That might be the easiest way to go about it," Garrison suggested.

Not only was his suggestion the easiest way to check the two against each other, but hearing the two read aloud only served to emphasize their similarities. While there were occasional differences in wording, the published article being the more smoothly written, the hypothesis in each was identical as was the support offered for it. When they finished, their eyes locked.

"This is no coincidence. This a clear case of plagiarism," Claire said flatly. "But who was copying whom? Surely Sydney Andrews wouldn't have submitted someone else's work as his own because . . ." Frowning, Claire's voice trailed away as she considered that possibility.

"Why not?" Garrison prompted.

"If plagiarism could be proved, that would be the death knell of his professional career. No professor would risk that." Claire's frown deepened. "Unless . . . unless he was scrambling to strengthen his publication record when he went up for tenure."

"Maybe there's a quick way to tell who copied whom. The second writer has to be the plagiarizer. This journal is the Spring 2004 issue. Is there a date on the Billingham paper?

Claire turned back to the front. "No. Like I said, there's not a cover sheet or even a title page. The paper starts with the title followed with his name centered below it."

Garrison frowned thoughtfully. "So what are our choices? Some student somewhere read the article in *The Oracle* and copied—"

"But if Billingham has no connection with this school, how did Rhodes get his paper?" Claire interrupted.

"Right. And that brings us to choice number two. As you suggested, Andrews, needing to improve his publication record, submitted a student's work as his own." Forestalling Claire's objection, he hastened to add, "I know, I know. It's not likely, too risky, could ruin his career, but it's possible. Of course, there's still the question of how Andrews got the paper since no Haskell Billingham has ever been enrolled at OSU. And I don't have an answer for that."

Claire was surprised she did have an answer. "But I do. This isn't the only place Sydney's taught. Before coming here he worked at a school in western Kansas. Billingham might have been a student there."

"Possible . . . possible," Garrison agreed. "And he could have run across that journal somehow and saw what his former professor had done. So he wrote to Dr. Rhodes charging Andrews with plagiarism and even sent his paper to support his claim. But why did he contact Rhodes instead of Dr. Larkin, the department head?"

"Maybe because it had been published in *The Oracle*, and Dr. Rhodes was the editor, that coupled with the fact that both the journal's editor and the plagiarizer were at the same school." Claire warmed to the possibilities. "Billingham probably thought Rhodes would take offense that such a prestigious journal had been used in this way and would do something about it. And that's why this paper was in Dr. Rhodes' briefcase," Claire announced triumphantly. Then her face fell in dismay. "All of which only proves Sydney's lack of professional ethics; it doesn't prove he killed Dr. Rhodes."

"No, but it does give Sydney Andrew a strong reason for being in Rhodes' office when he shouldn't have been."

"So are you going to arrest him," Claire asked eagerly.

"Unfortunately, knowing the motive for a murder isn't the same as proving beyond a shadow of a doubt that a person acted on it. Geraldine Kosvoski is proof of that."

Claire winced at the Kosvoski reference. Because of her, for a time Geraldine had appeared to be the killer. She had been wrong about Geraldine just as she had been wrong about George Karns and David Stands, and she had come within an ace of adding Rob Rhodes to her list of innocent suspects. Having a reason did not automatically make a person a killer.

"I've steered you wrong so many times, I hope I'm not doing it again," she said, slipping Billingham's paper back into the folder and handing it to Garrison as he returned the copy of *The Oracle* to her.

"That's all right," he said as the two stood and prepared to leave the office. "You've given me someone else to take a hard look at. Without your help I would never have made the connection between Billingham's paper and that journal article. I didn't know *The Oracle* existed."

Claire smiled at the compliment as he helped her with her jacket. "What do you need to cinch the case?" she asked as they walked down the stairs to the ground floor.

"A confession would be nice, but I doubt Andrews would willingly supply that. Billingham must have sent a letter along with that paper. Having that would make it clear how Rhodes got his paper, and it might even suggest what Rhodes intended to do with the information, or at least indicate what Billingham wanted him to do."

"So there wasn't a letter from him in Rhodes' briefcase?"

"No. Only the paper, your book, and the curriculum vitae for the four people up for some sort of personnel action."

"And Rob hasn't found a letter from Billingham at his father's house either."

Garrison looked at her sharply. "How do you know that?"

"I asked him."

"Why?" His tone was as sharp as his look.

"The same reason you want to see it," Claire said, surprised at Garrison's sudden change of mood. "I thought it might explain why Dr. Rhodes had Billingham's paper. He hasn't found it, but he said he'd keep on looking. Don't worry. If it turns up, I'll bring it right to you, okay?"

"Okay" was the brief answer. Garrison seemed preoccupied.

"Now, what I want to know is, what's next?" Claire grinned at him, trying to lighten his mood.

"A lot of police work, I'm afraid. It's good Andrews doesn't know you've made the connection between that journal and Billingham's paper."

"He doesn't know I've seen the paper but he does know I have that copy of *The Oracle*. He came into the

English office while I was checking it out and saw what I was doing."

Garrison's face clouded. "Does he know why you were taking that particular journal?"

"I told him I was impressed that he was published there and wanted to read his article."

"And did he believe you?"

"I guess so. I don't know why not. I really was impressed. That's a tough journal to get published in. Why do you ask?"

"The same reason I was concerned if Stands could trace my interest in his jacket back to you. If Andrews knew you were on to him, you might not be safe."

Garrison's statement knocked the grin from Claire's face. That was something she had not considered. Grant saw her shocked expression as he held the outside door open for her, and he hastened to reassure her.

"Since Andrews doesn't know you've seen Billingham's paper, you don't need to worry. This plagiarism lead is a big help, and I'd never have discovered it if it hadn't been for you. Thank you, Claire," he said before turning toward his car.

That's the first time he's called me by my given name, Claire thought as she bent her head against a stiff north wind on her way to the north parking lot. With the wind at his back, Garrison hurried to his vehicle parked on Morrill Avenue. Protected from that wind, a dark figure, which had moved silently down the staircase well behind the two, stopped just inside the east door of

Morrill Hall and stared though the glass panes at the re-
treating back of the police captain, who carried a
manila file folder.

*Blast! He let her see that paper. But the letter must
not have been in Rhodes' briefcase. It wasn't in his office, so it must be at his house. I can't try there again,
not since Garrison let that son keep his gun. I've got to
get that letter. Do I dare gamble he won't see the sig-
nificance of it if he finds it? But he's been hanging
around Claire. If he finds it and shows it to her, little
miss nosey might put two and two together. That's a
chance I can't take!*

Chapter Twenty-one

Over the weekend the weather remained on the chilly side of brisk, but nothing in the forecast heralded a white Christmas for central Oklahoma, much to Claire's disappointment. She remained indoors working at her apartment. She considered putting up a small Christmas tree but didn't. That was something she and Dirk might do together, she decided, before they went to her folks' in Wichita for Christmas day.

By Sunday evening, her apartment gleamed and the three late research papers were graded with only a modest penalty for their tardiness. She was ready for both finals week and Dirk. She was also ready for a phone call from either Rob or Grant, but as the weekend drew to a close, she heard from neither. She had hoped Rob would call to tell her he'd found a letter from Haskell

Billingham, but she was disappointed. Either he hadn't found such a letter or he had forgotten to look. She had also expected a call from Grant updating her on his investigation of Sydney Andrews. Again, another disappointment, and this one stung a bit. When they had left Morrill Hall Friday night, she'd felt like they were a team, working together on Dr. Rhodes' murder. But if he had made any progress on that case, he wasn't sharing it with her. Granted, she had to admit to herself, she wasn't on the police force; Grant was under no obligation to tell her anything. In fact, he had no business telling her what he had already, but they had seemed to be working together, and being left out hurt.

Monday brought both a break in the chill and the beginning of the final testing period. And Wednesday would bring Dirk back from Rome and into her arms, Claire thought happily. His flight would arrive at Oklahoma City's Will Rogers airport at 7 o'clock that midweek evening, and Claire was counting the hours. Fortunately, she was scheduled to give her tests on the first three days of finals week. She determined if she were really diligent and worked very hard, she could have most of her grading finished by the time Dirk arrived. There would still be final course grades to calculate, but she had until Saturday morning to complete that chore and turn in her grade sheets.

Monday morning also brought the *Tulsa World*. STILL NO ARRESTS IN PROF'S MURDER read the front-page headlines. At least this time they were below the fold, Claire noted. Apparently the OSU captain wasn't making his investigation of Sydney public yet. While her American Novel class filled their blue books with their answers to her three essay questions, she read the article, which she knew was deeply disturbing Grant Garrison. Beneath its thin veneer of journalistic objectivity, the article pointed out that the Oklahoma State University police force had spent three weeks investigating the murder of Dr. William A. Rhodes and had nothing to show for it. Although the article didn't say so directly, the implication was that if the crime were to be solved, the OSU force needed to step aside and let a real investigative body handle the case. The article concluded with a quotation from the public information officer for the Oklahoma State Bureau of Investigation saying the Bureau would willingly act in whatever capacity was required.

Claire considered phoning the beleaguered captain. There must be some good reason why he hadn't arrested Sydney. Perhaps he'd found a flaw in the case against the American lit professor as he had with all the other leads she had called to his attention. *He must really be down,* Claire thought and recalled him saying that words of encouragement were always appreciated. But what sort of encouragement could she give him? "Hang in there" or "You can do it" sounded hollow and insincere. Yet he had bent the rules and let her see the Faulkner paper found in Dr. Rhodes' briefcase. Friday night the case had seemed all but solved. Something must have happened. Curious what it might be and certain he needed some verbal support, she made the call as soon as she returned to her office.

"I saw the article in the Tulsa paper this morning. It was uncalled for and unfair, and it certainly didn't belong on the front page. If the paper felt the need to print it, it should have been in the opinion section," she told him warmly.

"Yeah, along with all the other editorials that have been calling for my scalp. A policeman's lot is not a happy one," he said, trying to make light of his predicament. "Nor is it a very speedy one. Building a convicting case takes time."

"And the OSBI couldn't have moved any faster!" Claire asserted with indignant heat.

"Actually, without your help connecting that paper to Andrews and giving him a motive, they probably wouldn't be this far along. I really do appreciate your help, and I wish I could be more specific about the investigation, but I can't. I hope you understand. I'm doing everything by the book. I don't want some leak or careless slip on my part to give Andrews a chance for an acquittal. When I make an arrest, it's going to be airtight."

"And I'm sure it will be. Until then, don't let the papers get to you."

"I won't. And thanks for the kind words. I appreciate them, especially when you have other more important things on your mind."

"Other things?"

"Isn't this the week your fellow arrives?"

"Yes, it is. How did you know?"

"You mentioned it when you were telling me about him."

"When—"

"After Dr. Rhodes' funeral. When we were having coffee."

"Oh. That's right. I guess I did run on about him. Yes. His plane gets in at seven Wednesday evening, and I'll be there with bells on."

"I'm sure you will. And thanks for the good thought. Take care of yourself, Claire," he said quietly just as he broke the connection.

Claire hung up the phone slowly. That was the second time he'd called her by her given name. Maybe they were on a first-name basis now.

Tuesday morning Sydney Andrews was still at liberty, and the newspapers were still demanding Garrison's removal from the case—no surprise there. What was a surprise occurred as Claire was returning to her office from her Survey of American Lit final. She did a double take and nearly dropped her armload of tests when she met Geraldine Kosvoski in the hall. She almost didn't recognize the woman. The lank, mousey brown hair was attractively cut, highlighted, and styled. For the first time since Claire had known her, Geraldine was wearing makeup, and Claire realized the woman had high cheekbones and the dark eyes under heavy, now well-shaped brows were slightly slanted. Her new pantsuit showed off both her waist and full bustline. Under the shapeless cardigans she usually wore, Claire hadn't realized she had either a waist or a bust. Geraldine was tall and solid, but she was more than just robust; she radiated a raw sexuality.

"Looking good, Geraldine. I love your hair," she said, hoping she wasn't gaping at the transformation.

Geraldine smiled at the compliment and waved her thanks before walking into the main English office. As Claire passed the door, she heard a masculine voice say appreciatively, "Well, hello, Geraldine!"

Claire grinned to herself. The departmental ugly ducking had just become a swan. On her way to her office, she noticed Elaine Evans' door was open, and as she stopped to greet her friend, Elaine motioned her in.

"Claire, have you seen Geraldine this morning?" she asked excitedly.

"Yes, just now. She's really taken herself in hand. I almost didn't recognize her."

"Yeah, me too. Do you think that improvement might have something to do with that son of Dr. Rhodes, who's still here in town? Jack and I saw them together having dinner at Chili's Saturday night."

"Really? Maybe so," Claire responded, frowning. She had warned Rob to be careful of Geraldine. She thought there had been too many recent romantic reversals in Geraldine's life and that the woman was vulnerable. But the woman she had just met in the hall looked far from vulnerable. She looked perfectly capable of taking care of herself. Maybe that was something she and Rob had in common—the ability to move from one partner to the next with surprising ease and haste. Then Claire's frown melted into a grin. "Well, that'd be good. Heightwise at least they appear to be made for each other." And perhaps temperamentally they were a fit too, Claire thought.

"Of course, I suppose she's still under suspicion until Dr. Rhodes' killer has been found. Although I have heard the police have backed off her as a potential murderer, but no one seems to know why," Elaine added.

That bit of news didn't surprise Claire. She knew why Grant was looking elsewhere for the killer, and he apparently was being discreet about why Geraldine was no longer a prime suspect. Claire could be discreet too, and Elaine would stay uninformed. Maybe Lee Burrows could keep his secret awhile longer.

Elaine looked at her friend with a worried smile. "I just hope the investigation doesn't go full circle, and they come back to you again, Claire."

That jarring thought made Claire flinch. Had Grant hit some sort of snag? Was that why Sydney hadn't been arrested yet? Was the leap between plagiarism and murder too difficult to make? Maybe Grant couldn't prove that being guilty of one made Sydney guilty of the other. And what might happen if the OSBI got the case? Since every other lead had turned up empty, would the fact that Rhodes' briefcase, which contained her book, was found in her locked office and her name was in his appointment book bring the investigation back to her? Unlike Grant, the OSBI might not find it convincing that the deceased professor had admired her work and that his hidden briefcase could be explained with the missing master key. Grant knew she was innocent and would defend her, she told herself forcefully. But a short time later, as she sat in her office grading tests, Claire's confidence that her innocence was firmly established would begin to crumble.

Chapter Twenty-two

The sharp rap on the frame of her open office door caused Claire to look up from the blue book before her and into the expressionless faces of the two men who filled her doorway. Both were wearing dark suits, white shirts, and ties, which immediately set them apart from most of the male faculty and all the male student body.

"Yes? May I help you?" she asked.

"We hope so," said the taller, more heavyset one of the two as he stepped into the room. He was followed by the slightly shorter, younger man. "I'm Captain Joseph Adams of the Oklahoma State Bureau of Investigation, and this is Lieutenant Warren Wheelwright." Both men produced wallets and flipped them open briefly. Claire caught a quick glimpse of badges and identification. The wallets disappeared back into their suit jackets as rapidly as they had appeared.

Rather than asking them to sit, as she normally would have done, Claire rose to her feet, spurred upward by a sudden shiver down her spine. Captain Adams continued.

"We'd like to ask you a few questions regarding the death of Dr. Rhodes, if you don't mind."

"All right," Claire answered hesitantly. "Has Captain Garrison turned the investigation over to the OSBI?" If he had, would her innocence be in question once more? she wondered, and a second shiver quickly followed the first.

"The OSBI is helping with the investigation," the captain answered smoothly.

Claire frowned. She knew that agency had been helping the campus police with lab work, but she hadn't realized their assistance had extended any further.

"I've already been interviewed by Captain Garrison. Surely you're aware of that. I've told him everything I know, which is very little." She attempted a small smile, and she felt her lips tremble. She was more nervous than she realized.

"Then you won't mind answering a few more questions," the younger officer interjected coldly.

His menacing tone sent another chill down her back. But it was more than his tone that bothered her. Both men were completely expressionless. She felt as though she were talking to two automatons.

"You were scheduled for an appointment with Dr. Rhodes the day following his death. What was the purpose of that appointment?" the older man asked.

"As I told Captain Garrison, I don't know. Dr. Rhodes only said he wanted to see me. He didn't say why."

"And you didn't ask?" Wheelwright interjected, his voice close to accusatory.

"No. I didn't talk to him. He'd had the departmental secretary put a note in my mailbox saying he wanted to see me after my morning class that Tuesday."

"And Dr. Rhodes' briefcase was found in your possession," Captain Adams said, resuming the direction of the inquiry.

"His briefcase was in my office, but not in my possession," Claire replied. A fourth chill rapidly coursed down her spine.

"You make some distinction?" the younger man asked.

"Yes, I do. I didn't know it was here. 'Possession' implies awareness; it suggests I knew the briefcase was here."

"Here being in that fireplace?" Adams asked for confirmation.

"That's where it was found—behind the logs."

Adams took a step backward and looked at the fireplace.

"It's not that difficult to see into the firebox. But you insist you were unaware of its presence?"

"At the time of Dr. Rhodes' death my office was a mess. It was very cluttered," she corrected. "I was still unpacking. There were boxes of books stacked in front of the fireplace that blocked it from view. I'm sure that whichever one of Captain Garrison's men who found it will corroborate that."

"We also understand that a book you had written was found in that briefcase."

"That's right. And did Captain Garrison also tell you that Dr. Rhodes had made some complimentary notations in it?"

For the first time Captain Adams' changed expression. Surprise quickly flickered across his face. Before he could answer, Wheelwright broke in.

"We'll need a sample of your handwriting, Dr. Markham."

"Okay. Sure. What do you want me to wr—" Claire had started to reach for her pen, but her hand wavered, and instead of a pen, she picked up the phone. She quickly punched in Grant's number. "But first I need to check with Captain Garrison. You don't mind, do you?" she asked, wondering why she hadn't done this before when the men had first identified themselves as OSBI agents. As the phone rang, she noticed the two exchanged a sharp glance. The younger man started to move toward her, but his superior stopped him with a slight negative nod.

The OSU police receptionist answered on the first ring.

"This is Dr. Markham in the English department. I need to speak with Captain Garrison right now. It's important." Her message was underscored by the tension in her voice, and her call was quickly transferred.

"Yes, Claire. What is it?"

Hearing Grant's voice bolstered her weakening confidence.

"I'm sorry to bother you, but I have a question. Have you turned the Rhodes investigation over to the OSBI?"

"No. Not that they're not eager to take it over. Why?"

"There are two OSBI agents in my office right now—a Captain Adams and Lieutenant Wheelwright. They're asking me questions and want a sample of my handwriting," Claire answered, now feeling confident enough to scowl at the two men, who were beginning to move toward the door.

Garrison's first response was a low oath muttered under his breath. His second response was louder and meant to be heard. "Don't answer their questions and don't give them a sample of your handwriting. They are acting beyond their authority. I'll be right over."

"They probably will be gone by the time you get here. They're already heading for the door," Claire replied before hanging up.

At the door Captain Adams turned back to Claire.

"It's just a matter of time before we have the case. And when we do, your lack of cooperation will be duly noted," he said before turning on his heel and leaving. The cold steel in his voice sent a flood of chills racing down Claire's back.

* * *

Claire was right; although Garrison arrived in Morrill Hall quickly, the two OSBI officers were gone.

"Why were they here?" she asked Garrison.

"They think I'll be forced to turn the case over to them, and they were just trying to get a running start," he answered grimly.

"They implied that I knew Dr. Rhodes' briefcase was here, and, of course, that also implied I'd put it here, which means they think I took it from his office after I killed him. And they knew a copy of my book was in the briefcase. When I said you'd found some complimentary notes in it, that's when that Wheelwright person asked for a copy of my handwriting, and I got spooked and called you."

"And I'm glad you did. They had no business being here. They were exceeding their authority, but my guess is they received an anonymous note about your book, just as I did."

"You got an anonymous note? About me?" Claire gasped.

"Two of them, in fact." Garrison smiled at Claire's startled surprise. "The notes suggested Dr. Rhodes had found something remiss with your scholarship. And, as I know from his marginal notes, that wasn't the case— just the opposite, in fact. But apparently the anonymous informer thought I wasn't acting on that information and alerted the OSBI too."

"So what were those two going to try to do? Prove that I wrote the compliments in order avoid having a motive for murder? If so, that's just stupid. Why would I go to that trouble, when I could have simply removed the book? No one would have known it had been in the briefcase. It wasn't necessary for me to forge anything." Claire stopped and looked at Garrison closely. "Grant, do you want a sample of my handwriting too? Just to be sure?"

"Thanks, but I don't need it. I've seen Rhodes' handwriting, and the margin notations were his. Should those two come back, or for that matter anyone else from the OSBI, call me immediately. Now, I'd better check to see if Adams and Wheelwright have been talking with anyone else without authorization."

After Garrison left, Claire tried to return to her grading, but she couldn't keep her mind on the tests before her. She was disturbed by the news of the anonymous notes, notes sent to both Grant Garrison and the OSBI, notes attempting to tie her to the murder of Dr. Rhodes. Who would do such a thing? Who would accuse her? Had she some unknown enemy on the faculty? she wondered. Someone who disliked her enough to try to pin a murder on her? As she sat lost in that troubling thought, the red ballpoint slipped from her fingers and fell unnoticed onto the opened but unread blue book. Claire stared into space, slowly sifting through the English faculty, analyzing each person, searching for the one who considered her capable of murder. Or could it be even worse than that? Could that person know she was innocent but see her as some sort of professional threat and this as a way to remove her? Or if not a professional threat, did the real killer see her as a handy scapegoat? Was Sydney Andrews trying to set her up? Possibly, and Claire mentally underscored his name. But if she was wrong and the notes weren't from Sydney, then who were they from? Maybe her enemy wasn't someone on the faculty after all. Sue Gooden, the departmental secretary, held her responsible for her breakup with Sydney. Might she be doing this in an attempt to get rid of a perceived rival? That was a possibility. Everyone in the department was a possibility, if you stretched things far enough, Claire realized. And once more she ran through the list of the faculty, reviewing her colleagues one by one. As she did, she became more and more angry and indignant.

"How dare anyone accuse me!" she fumed under her breath. "Just because Dr. Rhodes' briefcase turned up in here shouldn't make anyone jump to conclusions and go running to the police. If I'd taken the blessed thing, I sure wouldn't have crammed it in the fireplace, and I'd have had all Tuesday to get rid of it. How could anyone think—"

Claire stopped in mid-tirade, struck with a very uncomfortable realization. She was furious at someone who had only done what she herself had been doing, not once but three times. She was the one who had sent Grant Garrison searching the local landfill for David Stands' jacket. She was the one who had implicated either Geraldine Kosvoski or George Karns by insisting

Rob take the G. K. notes to the captain. She was the one whose curiosity had found a motive for Sydney Andrews. No. No one had a vendetta against her. If anyone jumped to conclusions, it was she. Granted, she had acted out of a desire to help find Dr. Rhodes' killer, nothing more. And whoever had written to Garrison and the OSBI could have been motivated by the same desire. However, just as she had been made to feel distraught by the false accusation of murder, so had she made David, Geraldine, George, and most recently Sydney, feel. They were no more guilty than she was.

Claire was not proud of herself, even though she had acted sincerely and without malice. So had the person who had written the notes naming her. Shamefaced, she picked up her red ballpoint to resume grading. As she did, she noticed the time. It was almost 12:45. She had let the morning get away from her with her pointless examination of her fellow faculty members. If she were to get the bulk of her grading done before Dirk arrived tomorrow evening, she couldn't waste any more time, especially since she had one more test to give tomorrow morning. She'd make a quick trip to the Student Union for a carryout sandwich to eat at her desk while she continued working.

Claire hurried back to Morrill Hall from the Union cafeteria carrying a tuna fish sandwich and a Diet Coke. Citing her need to continue grading, she had politely refused Elaine's invitation to join the crowded table of lunching English professors. And although it was true she needed to work, it was even more true that right now she found it uncomfortable to face the individuals she had erroneously directed to Grant Garrison's attention.

Chapter Twenty-three

By late afternoon the bread crumbs from the tuna fish sandwich had long since hardened and the last two swallows of the Diet Coke had grown warm in the can. Claire had been grading steadily since returning from the Union, and she wasn't yet finished with this set of tests. Badly in need of a break, she put her red ballpoint aside with a sigh and stretched hugely, her neck popping faintly as she rolled her shoulders.

A soft voice across the room caused her to start in surprise. Standing in the doorway, leaning against the frame with a broad shoulder was Rob Rhodes, who, from the amused look on his face, had been watching her for some time.

"Good grief, woman, you can concentrate. Are those

tests all that fascinating?" he asked with a devastating grin.

"Some more so than others. Come on in and have a seat," Claire invited, happy to have a reason for not immediately returning to work. "What are you doing up here?"

"I'm waiting on Gerry. She's in seeing Dr. Larkin."

"Surely not about your father, is it? I heard the police no longer consider her a suspect. Apparently her visit with Captain Garrison went well." *And things must be going very well between the two of them,* Claire thought, noting that Rob called the world lit prof Gerry rather than Geraldine.

"Very well, especially since Lee Burrows was there with her."

"So she's off the hook?"

"Looks like it—both with Garrison and with the university."

"With the university? What do you mean?"

"She's resigning. That's why she's in seeing Larkin."

"She's resigning!" Claire exclaimed, gaping at the news.

"Effective as soon as she's turned in her semester grades."

"Why? Whatever for?"

"The uncertainty of the whole tenure process is one reason. She thinks she'll be denied, and she's quitting before the committee can act. A sort of preemptive strike, as it were."

"You said 'one reason.'" Claire's green eyes narrowed. "That sounds as though there's another reason."

"Ah, there is. She needs to spend some time in Italy doing research—something dealing with Dante, I think she said. I happen to have business in Italy. She wants to go, and I want to take her."

The news that Geraldine wanted to do research in Italy didn't surprise Claire. Lack of a strong publication record was the main strike against her in the tenure process. But her leaving for Italy with Rob was so sudden that Claire was suspicious.

"You aren't just using her, are you, Rob?" Claire asked with concern for her colleague, even though she feared doing so would make the tall man angry.

Instead, the lazy smile turned into a wide grin, and he chuckled knowingly. "It could be she's using me. Ever think about that?"

She hadn't, and his question brought her up short. She tried a different tact.

"And have you considered the fact she had an affair with your father?"

The chuckle developed into a laugh. Not only was Rob not taking offense at her suggestion, he was amused by it.

"I'm not Oedipus, and Gerry's not my mother. Besides, she didn't love him. She saw their affair as a business arrangement. Unfortunately for her, Dad wasn't willing to pay off."

"And her affair with Lee Burrows?" Claire pressed.

"She's a healthy woman. Healthy women have needs that do not always involve the heart. But not you, Claire. You're one of those women where the two have to go together, love and sex. Dirk's a lucky man."

"And I'm lucky too. I appreciate your telling me about Dirk. A woman can't help but wonder, especially when you've been apart and he's around so many beautiful actresses," she murmured.

"You have nothing to worry about on that score. You can hold your own with any actress. As far as Gerry and I are concerned, let's put it this way: She's taken my measure, I've taken hers, and both of us are comfortable with what we found."

Okay, Claire, she told herself. *Back off.*

"That sounds fair, and I'm sorry for prying. But I do have one more question. Not a personal one!" she hastened to add as his eyebrows shot up. "Have you found a letter yet either from or maybe about Haskell Billingham in your father's things?"

"No, and since you mentioned it, I've looked. I've been though everything at the house and in his office, here. The only place I haven't searched is Dad's safe-deposit box. I can't. Tim, my oldest brother, is the executor of Dad's estate, so he's the only one with access to that, and he won't be back in town until after Christmas." He looked at her closely. "Although I suppose he could come earlier if it were necessary. Would this letter be important enough that Dad would have secured it in that way?"

Although Rob wasn't asking why such a letter would be important, Claire knew he wanted to ask. She was tempted to tell him but thought better of it. There were enough rumors in circulation, so she only answered the question he asked, not the one implied.

"It might have been that important. Or maybe not. I don't know."

"What don't you know, Claire?" A third voice joined the conversation as Geraldine Kosvoski walked into the room, and Rob rose in greeting.

Once more Claire was struck with the tall woman's transformation. Her black pantsuit was attractively cut and the lavender of her silk blouse was matched by lightly applied lavender eye shadow, which made her wide, high-cheekboned face both exotic and erotic. Although she was wearing heels, she still had to tip her face up slightly to receive Rob's affectionate welcoming kiss.

"I might have known I'd find you talking to a pretty woman," she said, clearly teasing Rob. "Now what is it you don't know, Claire?" she asked, repeating her question.

"I don't know how we're going to get along without you, Geraldine," Claire answered quickly. "Rob's told me that you've resigned."

"Sure did," the tall professor answered with a satisfied smile.

"What did Dr. Larkin say?" Rob asked.

"Several things." Geraldine smile broadened at the

memory. "That I was foolish to jump to conclusions regarding the outcome of my tenure decision, that I needed to really think through what I was doing, and that it wasn't professional of me to leave with so little notice."

Claire had been having similar thoughts, but this time she didn't voice them. What Geraldine and Rob did was their business. They were adults. Besides, the Junoesque world literature professor looked so happy and relaxed, Claire didn't want to ruin the moment for her.

"We'll leave you to your work now, Claire," Rob said as he slipped his hand under Geraldine's elbow. "We have an appointment with a realtor. Tim wants me to put Dad's house on the market and get rid of his furniture," At the door, he turned back and added, "When Dirk gets here, we should all go out for dinner."

"Okay. That would be nice," Claire answered. She watched the tall couple move out into the hall. In twenty-eight hours, she'd be walking with a tall, handsome man too. But until that time, she had one more test to give and grade and these to finish, and she opened the next blue book.

Late afternoon was fading into early evening as Claire drove north up Washington Street to her apartment. She glanced in her rearview mirror. A dark sedan was tailgating her. Tailgaters annoyed her. Stopping for the red light at Washington and McElroy, she checked the rearview mirror again. The sedan was still on her bumper. Claire continued north up the broad avenue. At the oddly angled junction of Washington and Boomer Road, she barely made the green light as she turned left. The dark sedan, sans green light, followed her through the intersection anyway and got honked at by a south-bound driver. The car was still right behind her at the red light at the corner of Washington and Lakeview. Claire frowned as she checked the mirror. The driver of that car was staring at her. Their eyes met in the rearview mirror, and Claire thought she had seen the man before, and recently too. She tried to place the im-passive face but early evening shadows made recogni-tion difficult. Even if she couldn't identify him, she could try to shake him, she decided. When the light changed, Claire sped away from the intersection, deter-mined to put some distance between herself and the tail-gater. The dark sedan sped up too, staying right behind her.

"Okay, maybe he just wants to drive fast. That's fine. I'll let him pass," Claire muttered to herself, and she de-liberately allowed her speed to drop. But even when her speedometer fell to fourteen miles an hour, the car didn't pass but remained on her bumper.

Suddenly Claire remembered where she had seen that hard, expressionless face. Yes, she had seen him recently—this morning, in fact—in her office. The driver of the dark sedan who was determinedly follow-ing her was Lieutenant Warren Wheelwright of the Oklahoma State Bureau of Investigation. In the fading light she hadn't recognized him sooner because he was unexpected and alone. The other agent, Captain Adams, wasn't in the car. But why was Wheelwright tracking her? Grant hadn't turned the case over to the OSBI. And he had instructed her to call him if anyone from that agency returned, and now Wheelright was back. His following her was obviously not a coincidence; it was deliberate. Claire felt a nervous surge in the pit of her stomach.

Nearing the wide drive into her apartment complex, she signaled a right turn, hoping the agent was not so close he couldn't see the blinking light. She didn't want him following her, but she didn't want him to rear-end her, either. The dark sedan slowed enough to avoid a collision and turned into the complex behind her. Claire drove around the circular drive and swung into her as-signed space. Wheelright stopped directly behind her car as though to prevent her leaving. Trying to show more bravado than she felt, she quickly stepped from her car and turned to confront the interfering officer. Remembering Captain Adams' threat when the two agents left her office, she hoped she looked more confi-dent than she felt. Her knees were trembling, but she lifted her chin in an attempt to look poised and defiant. Wheelright glared at her, his face no longer expression-less. He didn't speak; he let his hard stare communicate his message: "We've not forgotten you. We'll be back." Then he gunned the car away and left the complex. He had intended to intimidate her, and he'd been successful. Claire rushed to the door of her apartment and the phone inside.

If, during the drive from the campus, Claire had not been paying such close attention to Warren Wheelright and if the OSBI officer had not been so intent on following her, they might have noticed a third car, a dark blue Saturn, that tailed them both. The driver of the Saturn smiled as the two cars turned off Washington Street. The Saturn, however, didn't follow the two into the apartment complex. It proceeded on up Washington. The driver's smile widened and the bright eyes glittered.

Good. Someone's finally paying attention to my messages.

Chapter Twenty-four

Kaycee, sitting on the back of the couch, looked annoyed as Claire hurriedly entered the apartment. Once more Claire had disrupted their established routine; she was late and KayCee was tired of waiting for her supper. The calico cat, signaling her disapproval with a hiss, leaped lightly from the couch, stretched grandly fore and aft, and with tail erect marched into the kitchen expecting food.

Ignoring her cat's displeasure and insistent meows at the empty food dish, Claire hurried to the phone and dialed Grant's office number only to be told he had left for the day. She didn't have his cell number, and as she thought about it, she wasn't sure she would call him tonight even if she knew it. What could she say? Only that Lieutenant Wheelwright had followed and stared at her. He hadn't stopped her; he hadn't questioned her; he hadn't hung around the complex. If his presence had intimidated her that was her problem, not Grant's, she told herself. Grant had enough to worry about without her whining in his ear. If she saw him tomorrow, she'd mention it. She wouldn't bother him with it tonight. Besides, she had other things that needed attention, noting that KayCee's insistent meows had turned to strident yowls. Both she and her cat needed supper. And after supper, she had a stack of tests that needed her attention too, she thought with a sigh. Claire made sure her door was locked and got busy.

Wednesday morning Claire sat sipping a cup of coffee while her Children's Lit class worked on their final, the last test Claire had to give that semester, the last one she had to grade. Usually she didn't drink coffee in the classroom, but this morning was an exception. Caffeine was all that was keeping her bloodshot eyes open. Although she had finished yesterday's set of tests, grading until three in the morning had not been a good idea. Despite her exhaustion, thoughts of being followed by the OSBI agent and what that might portend had made it difficult for her to fall asleep when she did get to bed. The dark circles under her eyes testified to her lack of rest, and she had hoped to look her best when she met Dirk at the airport this evening. Maybe she could steal a quick nap this afternoon, she told herself.

Before leaving campus for that much-needed nap,

Claire took time to have lunch with Elaine at the Union, hoping she would see Grant there. She had tried to phone him when she arrived on campus shortly before the Children's Lit test, and once more he wasn't in. This time she left a message regarding her evening encounter with Lieutenant Wheelwright of the OSBI, and she was eager to learn if Grant had received it. *If I'd been able to reach him last night, I might have slept better*, she thought sourly, and it looked like she wasn't going to reach him at lunch today either. Captain Garrison was no where in sight.

In the large dining area, Claire and Elaine found a bigger gathering of English professors than usual. The finals week schedule had thrown the routine off a bit, and everyone had the same available lunch hour. Claire, remembering the anonymous notes sent to Grant and the OSBI, eyed the group uneasily, wondering if the person who wrote them was there; the people she had maligned were, she noted: David Stands, Geraldine Kosvoski, and George Karns. Even still-unarrested Sydney Andrews was there, which made Claire wonder if Haskell Billingham had been the plagiarizer after all and Sydney had no motive for searching Rhodes' office. She and Elaine were moving toward another table when Geraldine, today dressed in a stylish beige pantsuit, called to them. She nudged George Karns over so the two could join the group, whose conversation was focused, not on the unsolved death of Dr. Rhodes, but who would replace him as editor of *The Oracle*.

"Since manuscripts are being sent here, why can't one of us take over that editorship?" Sydney Andrews asked.

"For the obvious reason that the editorship was assigned to a person, not to an institution," Dr. Millington answered in a tone that suggested any fool should have known that. "The assistant editor, a fellow at the University of Illinois, will undoubtedly take over. He's a good man."

"But wouldn't it cause less paper shuffling and less confusion if—" Sydney began.

"There's going to be enough extra work this year as it is," Dr. McIntosh protested. "Until we can get someone hired, we've got to cover not only Dr. Rhodes' classes, but Geraldine's too, I gather." He shot a dark look at the wayward world literature professor, who smiled serenely back at him. "Your resignation is most sudden and unprofessional," he admonished with a scowl that was magnified by the thick lenses of his bifocals.

Geraldine was not in the least troubled by his complaints.

"Maybe Burrows will have to give up one of his under-enrolled linguistics classes and teach literature, for a change," she suggested blandly.

McIntosh ignored her suggestion and continued, "I suppose Larkin will divide up the theses and dissertations Rhodes was directing among those of us on the graduate faculty, as though we didn't have enough to do already."

"Well, I told Dr. Larkin I'm more than ready to help," David Stands interjected.

"Now that *is* a handy opportunity for you, David," Dr. Millington remarked, turning his sneer from Andrews to Stands. "Using a dead man as a ladder is one way of climbing into graduate teaching, isn't it."

Stands' face blazed with an angry flush, and he started to rise from his chair. "Are you suggesting—"

Dr. McIntosh hastily played the role of peacemaker and put a restraining hand on his arm. "No! Of course he isn't. We're all likely to say things we don't mean," he said with a sharp glance at Dr. Millington. "All of us are edgy and upset and will be until this business gets settled. Now, if the police would just . . ." His voice trailed off as he saw Captain Garrison moving toward their table.

"Sorry to interrupt," Garrison said to the group; then he turned to Claire, who expected him to mention receiving her call. What he said totally surprised her.

"I'll bring that Faulkner paper over to your office tonight," he announced, not lowering his voice, "but it will be seven before I can get there, I'm afraid. Oh, yes, and there's a letter I'd like you to take a look at too."

A strange combination of happy surprise and confused bewilderment quickly crossed Claire's face as she looked up at him. She knew what letter he meant. Somehow he'd found the one from Billingham, and she had to bite back the eager questions she wanted to ask. Talking about it in front of the English faculty wouldn't be smart, especially with Sydney sitting at the table. What she couldn't understand was why Grant was bringing the Faulkner paper back. He'd already let her see it. Besides, he knew where she'd be at 7 tonight, and it certainly wasn't her office.

"I don't understand. I won't be there tonight. I'll be—"

"That's right," he interrupted deftly. "I forgot. I still have Dr. Larkin's key, so I'll just leave them on your desk, if it's all right." And with a businesslike nod, he was gone before she could protest further.

Sydney Andrews looked at her closely, his eyes narrow slits.

"Something going on between you and the captain?" he asked.

"No! Of course, not. I thought he knew I'll be in Oklahoma City tonight."

"What's happening in Oklahoma City?" Geraldine inquired.

"My fiancé is arriving. We haven't seen each other for four months." Claire beamed broadly, anticipating the meeting.

"Then no telling when you'll get back to Stillwater," Sydney said with an insinuating leer. "I hope you're not supposed to give a final in the morning. You'd probably be too exhausted to get there."

"What a crude thing to say, Sydney!" Geraldine interjected before Claire could respond to his implication. "But then that's the sort of remark I'd expect from you. Not everyone behaves like you."

"Maybe not, but it takes one to know one, doesn't it, dear," Sydney answered with a nasty smirk.

Claire heard Geraldine's sharp intake of breath, but before she could respond, Dr. McIntosh broke in.

"Come, come! This is what I meant about all of us being under tension and saying things we don't mean. Now, has anyone heard anything about a search committee being formed to fill Dr. Rhodes' position?"

Dr. McIntosh's efforts at pacification were successful. Everyone was relieved to have something else to talk about, and the table talk turned to the subject of the impending job search and the technical writing professors' attempts to have that teaching slot assigned to them. Poor George Karns found himself the lone defender of that unpopular faction.

Glittering eyes covertly watched Claire as she finished her lunch, and a frantic mind raced.

I'd have thought the OSBI would have picked Markham up by now. They should have! Do I have to do everything? Apparently! And I need to do it quickly. So Garrison's going to be leaving both the paper and the letter in her office, and she won't be there. Interesting . . .

On the way back to her office after lunch, Claire stopped in the ladies' room. A quick look at her haggard face in the mirror convinced her she really did need a nap before meeting Dirk. Maybe an hour's rest would clear both her head and the dark circles under her eyes. She'd leave the final stack of test booklets at the office so they wouldn't clutter up her neat apartment, and after a short rest, she'd return to campus and continue grading until it was time to leave for the airport. So, rather than going back to her desk and the waiting tests, she left the building for the parking lot and her Mustang.

KayCee, this time curled up in the wing-back chair, looked up annoyed. This time Claire had arrived too early and interrupted her afternoon nap. To apologize for her lack of consideration, Claire stroked the cat's head, and as she petted KayCee, she noticed the flashing light on her answering machine. Assuming Garrison had called to tell her he'd received her message and to explain what he meant about leaving the Faulkner paper in her office tonight, she pushed the Play button, but it wasn't Grant who had left the message; it was Dirk. Her heart plunged when she heard his voice. Was it bad news? Had his departure been canceled? No, not canceled, but delayed by an East Coast snow storm. He'd still arrive in Oklahoma City tonight but not until 11:30. Claire was both relieved and disappointed: relieved they would be together tonight but disappointed their meeting would be delayed four and a half hours. But after four months, what difference would four more hours make? she told herself. That did mean she could take a longer nap, which was good because she feared one hour wouldn't be long enough to erase the dark smudges under her eyes, and she set her alarm for 5 P.M.

As she kicked off her shoes and stretched out on top of the bedspread, she wondered once more what Grant could possibly have been referring to in the cafeteria, but she was too tired either to call him or care. She had just settled into her pillow when KayCee jumped up on the bed. Not content to curl up at her side, the calico cat stepped lightly onto her stomach, treaded briefly, and then, using her mistress as a mattress, settled down to continue her interrupted nap.

At 5 o'clock, the alarm woke both the calico and Claire. And despite serving as a bed for an eleven-pound cat, Claire felt much refreshed and the circles under her eyes much diminished. As she smoothed the slightly rumpled bedspread, she recalled Grant's strange remark at noon. Her long nap had reawakened her interest in his cryptic comment. Why was he bringing the research paper back? She hadn't asked to see it again. But she did want to see the letter. Her curiosity demanded it. It had to be from Billingham, or if not Billingham, from whoever had sent the paper to Dr. Rhodes. Since she had no business seeing those things, Claire was confused. Why had Grant spoken to her in such a public way? She couldn't wait until 7; she wanted an explanation now. Although it was late, she called his office, but the receptionist said he wasn't available and asked, as usual, if she would like to leave a message. Claire thanked her but declined, leaving a message wasn't necessary. She would meet him at her office at 7; she'd be there grading, since her trip to Oklahoma City was delayed.

Claire filled KayCee's supper bowl and ran the vacuum one final time. As she put the sweeper away, she felt a faint fluttering in the pit of her stomach. She smiled. She really was excited to see Dirk. Or maybe she was just hungry. It was a long time until his arrival at 11:30, and she didn't like to evaluate student work on an empty stomach. Claire checked the refrigerator and spotted two slices of leftover meat loaf that needed to find a home. The cold meat loaf sandwich with mayonnaise and sweet pickles was both quick and tasty. After adding her plate to the few in the dishwasher, she started for the bathroom for a shower, but, to her surprise, the uneasy qualm still fluttered lightly in her stomach.

Not until she was standing in the shower with the hot water streaming over her did she recognize that little tremor for what it really was. What she continued to feel was a nagging discomfort caused by yesterday's threatening reappearance of the OSBI officer. She had left Garrison a message and had intended to mention it when she'd seen him in the Union during lunch, but he left so abruptly she didn't have time. Well, she'd be able to tell him about Wheelwright's appearance when he came to her office this evening, she decided, stepping from the shower.

A short time later, dressed in heels and the knit, bias-cut, long-sleeved dress she had bought for this re-union with Dirk, Claire checked herself in the mirror, happy with the choice she'd made. The dress clung in all the right places and the soft golden color was an attractive counterpoint to her shoulder-length auburn hair. She leaned toward the mirror to double-check her makeup and noted with satisfaction the well-applied base hid any lingering traces of the smudges of exhaustion under her eyes. She glanced at her watch and frowned. She should have settled for a two-hour nap. Sleeping for four hours had been a luxury she could ill afford. She needed to get to campus. The sooner she got busy, the more work she could get done before leaving for Oklahoma City. And if she intended to be there when Garrison arrived she needed to hurry. Claire was picking up her car keys when the phone rang. Thinking it was Garrison finally returning her call, she eagerly reached for the phone.

"Okay, so where did you find that letter you want me to see?" she asked as she picked up the receiver.

"I don't know anything about a letter, but I surely know I want to see you," a resonant, familiar voice rumbled in her ear.

"Dirk! I thought you someone else. But I'm glad it's you. Where are you?"

"New York, waiting for my flight. I wanted to be sure you'd gotten my message. I'm sorry I'm going to be so late, but this storm's slowed everything down."

"That's all right. I'm just glad you're finally going to get here. It's been so long."

"Too long. And it's not ever going to be this long again," he announced with feeling.

And as they continued their conversation, Claire forgot Warren Wheelwright and the uneasiness he'd caused her and Grant Garrison and his strange comment about the Billingham things. It wasn't until she left for her office in Morrill Hall and stepped out into the deepening darkness of the early winter evening that the slight flutter of tension returned.

Chapter Twenty-five

Claire pulled into the Morrill Hall lot and parked north of the building. For a moment she sat in her car, struck by the odd appearance of the old brick structure. The flutter in her stomach coiled into a knot. Something didn't seem right. Then she realized what was so unusual: all the windows were dark. Usually at this time, there were lights on in some of the classrooms and offices, but not tonight. Was the power out? she wondered. If it was she couldn't work here; but maybe she could grope around in the dark well enough to get into her office and pick up the tests to take home, she thought as she stepped from her car. However, when she walked around the corner of building on her way to the east door, she felt foolish. Her concern was unfounded. She had allowed Wheelwright's intimidating behavior to unnerve her, causing her to imagine problems where there were none. Bright light poured through the glass panels of the east door and through the tall window above it. The power wasn't out. All the hall lights were burning. She could work here as planned.

Claire loosened the long green scarf around her throat and unbuttoned her jacket as she stepped through the east door of Morrill Hall, but she stopped just inside the entryway, puzzled. Although the halls were ablaze with lights, the building was strangely quiet and empty. *That's odd,* she thought, frowning. Usually people were around in the evenings: students using the writing lab, graduate students going to a night class, professors returning to continue work. Where was everyone? Her apprehension returned, causing the hair on her forearms to prickle. For a moment she was tempted to leave the building.

Then her frown faded. Of course. No one was around because the only English test scheduled for tonight was the Freshman Composition final. She remembered Elaine saying the comp final was a common exam, which meant all the sections were taking the test at the same time. Consequently, in order to accommodate the number of students involved, the test was being given in the large lecture rooms in Ag Hall and the Animal Science buildings across campus, and Elaine was riding herd on things over there. That explained why no one was around, Claire thought, and she started up the stairs to her office, chiding herself for her nervousness.

But the echo of her footsteps in the empty building seemed ominous. It shouldn't be this quiet. Where were the janitors? They weren't giving the common exam. They should be here as usual emptying waste baskets and cleaning the restrooms, but they weren't. The hair on her forearms stirred again. At the landing in the turn of the long staircase, Claire paused and again considered leaving the oddly silent building. But once more she admonished herself for her discomfort.

"You're behaving like you're the last living cell in a dying body," she murmured aloud, trying to tease herself out of her nervousness. "Remember why you're here and quit wasting time." And with that she spurred herself on up the stairs to her office.

Quickly Claire unlocked her door, turning the key so it would lock behind her, and she stepped into the dark room. As the door closed, she reached for the switch and flipped on the overhead lights. Blinking against the sudden glare, she stopped with a gasp. Standing behind her desk holding a just extinguished flashlight and a sheaf of papers was Sydney Andrews. He appeared as startled as she. Claire was the first to recover her tongue.

"Sydney! What are you doing here?" she asked in shocked puzzlement.

"I could ask you the same. You're supposed to be in Oklahoma City."

"How did you get in?"

Sydney paused before answering, but there was no need to dissemble. There was no excuse he could make that would explain his presence in her office. Perhaps Claire deserved one final truth.

Now that she's here, she'll have to stay. But it was going to come to this anyway. The nosey broad. She has only herself to blame.

"The same way I got into Rhodes' office." He dangled the missing master key from a narrow leather strap.

"How did you get that?" Claire gasped.

Sydney smiled knowingly. "Secretaries can be such trusting, gullible little things. And handy too."

"I thought Sue didn't know about that key."

"She didn't. She didn't give it to me. She gave me something else, all right," he said, his smile changing to a leer, "but not the master key. It was Phyllis, the one before her, who mentioned it to me. But she never missed it." Sydney dropped the papers and key on her desk and moved deliberately around the desk.

Claire knew she was learning more than she should and began to edge away. Sydney quickly stepped between her and the door, cutting her off.

"I found the research paper, but the letter isn't here. Where is it?" he asked sharply.

"What letter?" Claire asked, playing dumb and also playing for time. She knew exactly what letter he meant. She also knew something else, and she swallowed hard at the thought. Garrison had already been here. She couldn't rely on him for help, she realized as she stared at Sydney. Behind those glittering eyes, Claire saw a desperate mind, an irrational mind. And she was desperate herself, but not irrational. She was going to have to get out of this on her own. No Dirk to her rescue this time. Maybe if she could keep Sydney talking, he'd let his guard slip, and she could get by him to the door. He was conceited enough it might work, she told herself.

"What letter?" he exclaimed. "The one Billingham sent Rhodes. The one Rhodes threatened me with."

"I don't know what you're talking about. I don't know anything about a letter," she lied, hoping she sounded convincing.

"But you do know about Billingham's paper, don't you? You and Garrison were up here with it, probably comparing it to my article. That copy of *The Oracle* is still here," Sydney said, gesturing to the journal she had left on the corner of her desk.

Claire opened her mouth to protest, but he curtly added, "Don't deny it. I saw you two leave."

"Yes, we did compare them. And I saw how Billingham had plagiarized you."

"You saw how Billingham had plagiarized me!" he exclaimed scornfully. "Oh, come on, Claire. You're not that stupid. And I'm not stupid enough to be taken in by your pathetic lie. You figured out what had happened, that I'd made rather free use of a former student's work."

"But you've never had a student by that name."

"No, not here. But I did at Fort Hays, when I taught in Kansas. And he was good. So good in fact, I made a Xerox of his term paper. Thought I might use it as an example of what graduate students could do; something for other students to aspire to."

"There was nothing wrong with that," Claire said, trying to mollify him.

"Maybe not with that, but that's not the whole story." Sydney smiled ominously. "Surely someone as curious as you wants to know the whole story."

Claire had the sudden image of a cat toying with a mouse before sinking its sharp teeth.

Sydney continued, "Instead of using that paper as an example to motivate others, I found I had another use for it. Publication counts so heavily here for promotion and tenure. With Rhodes against me, I needed to bolster my publication record. Besides, what did it hurt? Billingham was teaching in some rural high school out in western Kansas. He'd never know. And I'd have gotten away with it too, if somehow he hadn't blundered onto that issue of *The Oracle*. What's a schoolteacher in Hoxie, Kansas, doing reading *The Oracle*?"

"But how did Rho—" Claire started to ask.

"He wrote to Rhodes because he was the editor of *The Oracle*," Sydney interrupted, and he began once more to slowly move toward Claire, and she, just as slowly stepped backward. "And he charged me with plagiarism. He even sent the paper I had graded to support his claim. But if I could get his paper and letter, then neither he nor Rhodes could prove anything."

Despite herself, Claire was drawn in to his story. "But Dr. Rhodes confronted you, and—"

"Confronted me! That's putting it mildly. He gave me an ultimatum: resign by the end of the semester and leave the profession or he'd make it known what I'd done. And as the editor of *The Oracle*, he had the platform for it." Anger distorted Andrews' features. "He threatened to take away my livelihood! I couldn't let him do that."

"So you went to his office to search for the paper and letter, and he walked in on you. Just as I did now."

"And you know what happened in Rhodes' office."

Yes, she knew what had happened in Rhodes' office. And Sydney appeared to have every intention of repeating that with her.

"But surely it wasn't murder. It was self-defense or, in the heat of the moment, maybe manslaughter." Claire was scrambling to give him, if not an out, a way to lessen the charge against him.

The feral eyes glittered. "No, it was murder, all right. It didn't happen quite like I thought it might if I couldn't get those papers back, but it happened. And now you know too much, and it's going to cost you."

"But why? What will that accomplish?" Claire's voice was shrill with tension. "Billingham's still out there, and the police have his paper. Garrison's already suspicious of you." She fought to control her voice. "If anything happens to me, it will just cinch his case against you."

"But I've already killed one person. So what's one more body? I can only be executed once. If it hadn't been for you, I would never have been suspected. You're going to have to pay for that!"

The cat struck, and Sydney suddenly reached for Claire. As he closed in on her, she ducked and spun around him toward the door. He clutched at her arm, but she twisted away, and his fingers slipped from the sleeve of her leather jacket. She reached the door and groped for the knob. From behind, he grabbed the long scarf looped around her neck and pulled her backward into his chest. His fists twisted her scarf shorter, and, despite her struggles, he pulled the scarf tight against her throat and tighter still.

"This is better than a letter opener," he whispered, his mouth against her ear. "No blood on me. No air for you!"

Claire jerked back and forth trying to force her fingers under the scarf to drag it away from her throat as the pressure increased, but she couldn't. The scarf was too tight. Bright sparks blazed before her darkening eyes. The scarf pulled tighter. Claire slumped forward carrying her assailant to the floor with her as she began to lose consciousness.

She was unaware of the door banging into her head as someone attempted repeatedly to force it open. The angry voices were drowned out by the roaring in her ears.

"Claire! Claire! Can you hear me?"

Someone was calling to her, but the voice was far away and strange sounding. Suddenly a mouth covered hers, and oxygen rushed back into her aching lungs.

She gasped and coughed. The mouth moved. Someone slapped her cheeks, and a frantic voice called her name.

"Claire! Say something. Are you all right? If anything had happened—"

"Who—?" she croaked weakly.

"It's Grant. You're safe now. They're taking Andrews away. He's under arrest."

Everything seemed to be happening in slow motion as the world gradually came back into focus, and Claire realized she was lying on the floor in Grant Garrison's arms. She struggled to sit up, but the effort made her head swim, and she sank back.

"We'll get you to the hospital," he said cradling her.

"Just—get me to—a chair first," she rasped painfully.

Grant helped her to her feet and, holding her upright, hooked a fireplace chair with his foot, pulled it over, and lowered her into it.

"You need to see a doctor. Luckily that wool scarf was soft, but you have bruises on your throat."

Claire rubbed her tender throat slowly and discovered it hurt to swallow. The world still seemed a bit out of kilter, and an odd thought struck her as funny.

"Bruises—on my throat, huh?" she whispered hoarsely. "And I was worried about—circles under my eyes."

"Circles under—what are you talking about?" Grant's voice reflected the fear that oxygen deprivation had left its mark.

"Wanted to look my best for Dirk," she explained

weakly. Then the green eyes sharpened, and she pushed from her diaphragm to take the pressure off her throat. "Why are you here? You'd already left that paper." Claire's head had cleared. "*Why* did you leave that paper? I didn't ask to see it again."

"I did it to flush out the killer. You were right, Claire. Rhodes' murder was related to something in his brief-case. Whoever had gone after what was in it once before would be likely to do so again. I had to see who would show up."

"So you planted it in my office. I was the bait! You used me for bait!" she accused him huskily, jerking away from his comforting touch.

"No, I didn't. Not really. You weren't supposed to be here. You were supposed to be in Oklahoma City."

"Since you had Billingham's letter, you didn't need to wait to see who showed up. You knew who the pla-giarizer was. Why didn't you just arrest Andrews?"

"But I don't have a letter from Billingham."

"What? There was one. Rhodes showed it to An-drews. If you didn't have it, why did you tell me you wanted me to see a letter?"

"That was just a lucky guess, a spur-of-the-moment inspiration. I was trying to set the hook as deeply as I could. I figured a letter must have come with the paper, and whoever killed Rhodes would want it too."

"Why didn't you tell me what you were doing?"

"There wasn't time. It happened so fast, seeing all of you there at the cafeteria at noon. All the likely suspects were there. I just saw an opportunity and took it. I didn't want you to be any more involved than you already were. Besides, I thought you'd be at the airport."

"But I wasn't, and you let me walk in on Andrews," she accused bitterly.

"We didn't expect you. If we'd stopped you, it would have ruined everything. My men and I were nearby."

"Then why were you so long in getting here?" Claire demanded.

"You were talking. Andrews was confessing. I told you when I broke this case it was going to be airtight. I was letting him convict himself."

"Well, yeah. But he was telling me, not you."

"He was telling us too. We'd hidden a motion sensitive camera and microphone in your office."

"How did you expect that to work in a pitch-black office when he was in here by himself?"

"We were sure he'd have a flashlight, and if we were really lucky, he might have muttered to himself."

"So while you were busy monitoring the monitor, you very nearly let him strangle me," Claire accused.

"And for that, I'm truly sorry. Both of you were on the floor against the door. We had a hard time forcing it open. Now, come on, if you're not too dizzy to walk. I'm taking you to the emergency room." And without waiting for an answer, he helped her to her feet.

Claire stepped away from his encircling arm, staggered slightly but recovered her balance. "All right, but I'm leaving town no later than ten."

Grant frowned. "The hospital will probably want to keep you overnight, and I'll need a statement."

Claire's green eyes flashed. "Well, the hospital will just have to be disappointed, and so will you if it takes longer than ten o'clock. Dirk had to take a later flight, and his plane gets in at eleven thirty. I intend to be there. You got the man you want. And if you think you're going to keep me from getting the man I want, you are badly mistaken," Claire announced as forcefully as her sore throat would let her, and she started for the door.

Grant picked up her scarf from the floor where it lay and followed her. He couldn't stop her. She was going to get the person she wanted. He might have Dr. Rhodes' killer, but he didn't have the person he wanted, not really. The person Grant Garrison wanted was the slim, chestnut-haired woman with the bruised throat who was walking away from him on her way to the arms of another man. And from the set of her jaw, it was plain she wasn't going to let anyone stand in her way.